CIVILIZED SAVAGES

by Susan Kaye Behm

Llumina Press

© Copyright 2002 Susan Kaye Behm

Requests for permission to make copies of any part of this work should be mailed to Llumina Press, PO Box 772246, Coral Springs, FL 33077-2246 or to info@llumina.com.

ISBN: 0-9718509-6-8

Printed in the United States of America

DEDICATION

I would like to thank certain people for their encouragement in giving me the encouragement to write this book. A special thank you to Ella, Sharon, Linda, Francine and Dale. These special people as well as many many more are responsible for giving me the love and friendship I needed.

I would also like to dedicate this book to a very special friend, Debbi. The Lord sent her to be my friend when I needed a friend more than anything else in the world. Her consistency has been an incentive for me to keep on going. God has used her over and over again to sort of prop me up on the leaning side. Thank you.

For the White Family!
The horrible nature of abuse against the defenseless (as Christians) cannot be understood. As Christians we have an obligation to be protectors of God's children and we must work to save anyone from entering the never ending nightmare that abuse brings' together. We must stand together.

God bless you

SK Bahr

I Chron 28:20

June 10, 2006

Table of Contents

INTRODUCTION

Massive propaganda floods the area.

- The Evening Star

Millions in danger of losing their jobs....
Unemployment levels soar.

- The Global Sun

U.S. ECONOMY IN SEVERE RECESSION

People all over the country lose confidence in elected officials.
...clearly, the wretched state of the economy is only the immediate
element of a drama that encompasses nothing less than the
creation of an entirely new order on the ruins of the old.

- The State Journal

ATTEMPTS TO REFORM GOVERNMENT FAIL

The last guardians of the system failed
miserably in their attempt to restore an ideology
that had been dead on its feet for several years.

- The Patriot Journal

PRICES SOAR

This week, prices have soared out of government control.
The high-stakes crap game of radical economic reform will begin.
....many bone-weary shoppers begin the three-hour
lineup for milk and bread at 5:00 a.m.

- The City Review

HEALTH-CARE SPENDING REACHES ALL-TIME HIGH

One out of every five dollars in our economy will be spent for healthcare. ...reasons for the rapid rise of health-care costs include the increasing reliance by medical personnel on costly, high-tech equipment, new treatments of such illnesses as cancer, and the aging of the population, which means further increases in expenditures.

...with medical costs increasing, the pressure to do away with old or poor patients rises.

...doctors are giving lethal injections to patients without their consent in order to bring population growth under control.

...no repercussions against doctors for taking lives.

...leaders lean toward eliminating everyone deemed unfit.

- Military Guide

MILITIAS ARE BEING FORMED AROUND THE COUNTRY

Elected officials have lost the confidence of their constituents. Former military leaders are forming their sects nationwide. The entire population is going through an identity crisis.

- Blue Water Post

MILITARY LEADERS PROMISE A BETTER LIFE FOR ALL WITHIN ONE YEAR

Public opinion polls reveal that 79% of our citizens believe that, as bad as things are, worse times lay ahead.

- Eastern Journal

RUMORS PERSIST THAT CHILDREN WILL BE TRAINED FOR SPECIAL MILITARY DUTY

...Militia leaders have ruled that newborns in their sectors must be given genderless names.

...Any child under the age of seventeen having a gender-specific name must have it changed to comply with the new mandate.

- Town Post

PROLOGUE

Many of the various militias began sealing the borders of the areas that they control. The leaders censored any materials coming in and leaving their sector. Propaganda swayed the population into believing a national crisis existed thus setting a chain of events into motion unlike any other in history.

CHAPTER 1
WHAT OF THE CHILDREN

Winter had arrived and the snow began falling. The late-afternoon sun broke through the clouds enough to make everything glisten. A gentle breeze scattered loose snow into faint patterns on the ground. Snow fell as the families arrived, spotting the slumbering trees with a glistening coat of white. The scene would have been considered serene if it had not been for the unanswered questions about the children.

When the Militia announced that there would be a town meeting for the parents, they promised all of their questions would be answered. Families from all over the sector hurried to the meeting.

They were anxious to know what was going on. The families had been in an uproar for the six weeks since soldiers forcibly removed their children. They were powerless to do anything more than wait.

Due to military rule, the families were frightened of demonstrating too much disapproval. Any such outcry might bring violent repercussions, and many hoped the meeting would answer their questions. All they could do was sit and wait anxiously for the meeting to begin.

Finally, at six o'clock, the leader, Major Julius Doyle, a man of forty-five or so strode in. He was flanked by two adult guards and lastly, the children. His dress uniform and stern glance made him extremely intimidating. The people trembled in his presence.

The children were dressed in khaki fatigues and moved with robotic precision. Coming to a halt, they formed a line that stretched across the platform and onto the floor. At the sight of them, many of the adults in the audience gasped in horror.

The Major kept his back to the children and barked, "Attention!"

Instant obedience.

"Right face!"

Mechanically, they turned to face the audience.

Family members stared in shock, searching the children's faces. Their eyes were met with cold, empty stares. No signs of recognition. Each child's face was stoic with eyes staring blankly ahead.

"What have you done to them?" One woman shrieked, waving her fist.

"Good evening!" Major Doyle began, ignoring the woman. "I know many of you have inquired about your fine young people. First, let me assure you they're in excellent health and have proved a credit to you and to the Militia." He smiled with pride.

"These compatriots have just completed six weeks of intense training. Any explanations at the time would have been beyond your understanding. Now here is your explanation. They are physically stronger and mentally sharper than any of you here."

The parents and relatives stared at their children in horror, who did not so much as flinch as they stood at attention.

"I still don't understand!" Henry Benson, a white-haired, sixty-year-old laborer. He stood to his full six-foot height. His muscular body towering over those around him. "What have you done to my granddaughter, Josephine Benson?"

Other audience members began shouting questions until the din rose so no one could understand a word. The Major remained quiet until the roar of the crowd died down and there was silence.

Major Doyle took a long, hard look at Henry Benson, then said, "First of all, I believe you are mistaken about the name. I believe you mean Joey Benson."

"Sergeant Joey Benson, front and center," he ordered.

Joey stepped forward, her feet snapping as she turned right, then left. She stopped exactly in the center of the platform. Joey was only eleven but in her military uniform she seemed much older. It was true; Josephine Benson had been transformed into Joey Benson. Her long hair had been exchanged for a crew

6

cut; her brown eyes were empty; her body was more muscular than it had been; and her smile had long ago disappeared.

Henry gasped when he saw his granddaughter. He barely recognized her as the smiling girl with the ponytail he'd seen six weeks earlier. Dresses and patent leather shoes had been replaced by khaki fatigues and heavy black boots.

"What do you think, Mr. Benson?" Major Doyle asked. "You should be very proud of Joey. She excelled beyond her classmates and has already achieved the rank of sergeant. Competition was fierce, but she has proved herself worthy." He smiled in pride.

"What did you do to her?" Henry's teeth clenched. "That's not my little girl. You monster!"

Two guards moved quickly toward Henry Benson.

Major Doyle scowled. "She isn't YOUR little girl anymore. She's a loyal compatriot to this Militia. Any further outbursts or statements to the contrary will be considered resistance to the New Order. We do not look favorably on resistance. Now sit down, sir."

The edge on the Major's voice and the approaching guards made Henry shrink back in fear. Major Doyle surveyed the audience and smiled at his power.

"These young people are loyal servants of the Militia. . . ."

"You mean slaves, don't you?" Jason Burrows, a fifty-five-year-old office worker, spoke out. Jason Burrows became unemployed after the New Order took control of the town.

"What did you say?" Major Doyle barked in surprise that anyone would interrupt him after his warning.

"You indicated you all were the superior ones." Jason stood with his hands on his hips. "Or doesn't that include your hearing?"

"Who do you think you are?"

A guard moved to grab Jason Burrows, but Major Doyle waved him off. A sadistic smile crossed his face.

"My name is Jason Burrows. You kidnapped my nephew, Jesse Burrows, and I don't like this business. Jesse is only twelve years old. He's a boy, not a soldier. He should be out playing baseball, not preparing for a war."

"Corporal Burrows!" Major Doyle summoned.

"Yes, Sir!"

"Are you a boy or a soldier?"

"A soldier, Sir! Serving this Militia, Sir!"

"I see many of you don't understand our program." Major Doyle eyed the audience. "We took your young people, fed, clothed, and housed them, and gave them the finest training in the land. With the problems in the government, you should thank us, not defy us."

"Thank you my foot!" Jason lunged and grabbed Jesse's arm to pull him from the line. "I'm taking him home."

Jesse moved into a combat stance and waited for Major Doyle's order. Jason tried to force him to leave. Major Doyle nodded. Fists raised, punches flying as Jason pushed and pulled at Jesse. The older man struggled to move Jesse off the platform. Everyone watched without interfering. Jesse was winning the struggle.

Suddenly, Jason stepped back, clutched his chest.

"Cease, Burrows!"

Jesse obeyed immediately and stepped back into formation. Leaving his uncle slumped to the floor.

"So we have a weak heart, do we?" Major Doyle asked in mock sympathy. "According to our new regulations, this condition should have been reported to me a long time ago."

"Help me!" Jason begged.

"Now you cry to me for help? A moment ago, you defied me. I dare say, Mr. Burrows, you should think these things through before opening your mouth."

With a waive of a hand, several young people moved forward and formed a barrier around Jason. Facing outward, they took fighting stances, ready to attack anyone.

"Stay where you are!" Major Doyle ordered the parents.

They stared in disbelief. Determined not to let a friend die, several moved forward again trying to get near enough to help Jason.

"Company A, restrain!"

Twenty of the children ran forward to reinforce the circle around Jason.

Family members tried to push past the children to aid Jason Burrows but without success. The children formed a human wall. After several attempts, the adults were forced to stand by helplessly and watch Jason die. His cries of pain sent shivers down everyone's spines, but the children did not seem to notice. Within minutes, he was dead.

"Smith, Jackson, Roberts, Rogers, take the body to the recycling depot in the basement. Tell the handlers to hurry. After all, the poor are hungry." A smirk crossed his face.

Three boys and one girl stepped forward. They pushed through the crowd and lifted the limp body as if it were a rag doll. The eyes of their family members followed them, horrified at what they saw.

When Jason's body was carried out, the people turned their attention back to Major Doyle. Shock and disbelief left them unable to speak.

"That brings up another subject," the Major said. "We discovered the solution to our food-shortage problem."

Henry's face showed understanding of the horrible reality.

"I see you understood me, Mr. Benson. Why don't you explain it to the others?" The Major stood back and crossed his arms.

Everyone looked at Henry in confusion.

"He means . . . they're . . . ." Henry swallowed hard. "They're using the dead for food."

Gasps of horror echoed throughout the room. A few people clutched their stomachs and mouths and ran for the door.

Major Doyle smirked again. "I knew you were bright, Mr. Benson." He looked at everyone and saw fear in their eyes. "Formation!"

The children returned to their places on the platform.

"I trust that little demonstration leaves no doubt in anyone's mind what might happen if you dare resist our New Order. Let me caution you, none of you can defeat our superior warriors. Don't let your previous memories of them or your relationships with them fool you into thinking anything else. I'd hate to have them make you into an example.

"Tomorrow, our guards will visit you. They'll inform you of changes you must make to bring your household into compliance with our latest regulations in order for your young people to return home for visits. Your full support and cooperation is expected."

Fear is an effective tool for control. He saw it in their eyes as they considered the possibility of battling against their own children.

"One last announcement before I adjourn this meeting," Major Doyle said. "In order to maintain our level of superiority and power, we'll need a constant influx of young people into our program. Therefore, we'll review the papers of every woman between the ages of eighteen and twenty-five. On completion of these reviews, we'll interview them and select those we feel will give birth to the appropriate caliber of child.

"Those we select will go through an impregnation process. Afterwards, you'll remain in our dormitory for monitoring until the child is delivered or until we request termination of the pregnancy. This is not optional."

Everyone sat in shock. They could not believe these things were happening. Henry sat with the rest of his family, shaking his head in horror.

"Dismissed." Major Doyle smiled. There was no longer any reason to continue the pretense of kindness toward them. Those people knew the New Order for what it was when they saw a man die in front of their eyes. They had good reason to be afraid.

CHAPTER 2
TRAINING OR ABUSE

Early the next morning, the young soldiers rose, made their beds, and moved to the dining area for breakfast -- all without making a sound. No one mentioned the events of last evening. Yet, the expressions on the parents' faces haunted Joey's memory, especially the look in her grandfather's eyes. If anyone else was thinking about their parents, the death of Jesse's uncle, or anything else from last night, no one betrayed their thoughts.

Joey moved silently through the breakfast line, punched in her designated personal identification code, and received her specially prepared breakfast. She hated the new diets they'd forced upon her. The food was tasteless and had an unappetizing color. Joey studied the cup of pills that were now a regular part of her morning routine. The pills made her feel strange, but she was unsure of how to explain the feeling. Somehow all of it was supposed to work together to make her stronger and more alert. Every bite had to be consumed and every pill taken. Guards monitored them at all times and checked their food trays.

Taking her place at the dining table, she stared at her bland meal silently. The recruits fixed their eyes on their plates. Guards watched carefully, making sure no one's eyes wandered. During their first week of training, the instructors had drilled into them the fact that there was no time to socialize.

After the guards had removed her from her home, she had been delivered to the barbershop where her long hair was cut above her ears and collar. Next they had issued her several changes of khaki uniforms, a black belt, a green cap, and heavy black boots. The weight of the boots hurt her legs. At least

11

she did not face the problem of deciding what to wear each day. Physically, the little girl she had been six weeks ago was only a distant memory.

Girls and boys were treated the same. They shared the same barracks and bathrooms. Enforced equality was a fact of life. No one would admit that they were bothered by it -- no one dared to notice the obvious physical differences between them. It was safer to keep your focus short-sighted.

Joey glanced out of the corner of her eye at her compatriots. A little twinge of loneliness peeked out of the shadows, but there was no such thing as having a friend here.

Would things be different if I had a friend? I guess I had friends before, I can't really remember. Having a friend would probably be detrimental. Knowing the names of my compatriots is enough. It is safer that way. We have a job - to serve the New Order.

Over the past few weeks she had learned friendship was dangerous and a sign of weakness. She knew one had to guard against any appearance of weakness. The mere appearance could bring horrible repercussions.

After breakfast, each of them reported to the infirmary for daily injections.

Why do we need all these shots and pills? Joey wondered. *The Major says it's a vitamin supplement, but both the pills and shots make me feel funny. I don't think just vitamins would make me feel so weird.*

After the infirmary call, each young soldier returned to their various barracks. They were grouped by age and rank. Between the shots and the morning inspection, they had twenty minutes to put the finishing touches on their uniforms and cubicles.

In order to be ready if an officer came early, a lookout system had been established. Each took their turn, this day it was Joey's turn. She stood out of sight, prepared to warn the others of an approaching officer.

The rest of the group milled about and talked about the glory of the New Order. It was the only safe subject for conversation. They knew anything they said could find its way back to Major Doyle's ear.

"Attention on deck!" Joey hissed her warning and rushed into the room to take her place.

Everyone snapped to attention, all eyes fixed straight ahead. There were no snickers or smiles as Major Doyle marched into the room.

His perfectly-pressed dress blues stood in stark contrast to the khaki the children wore. There would never be a question about who was their leader.

He glanced at them, then walked up and down the aisles inspecting each more closely. It was a daily routine, and he would not tolerate even the tiniest infraction of the rules. The children had to be perfectly dressed -- all shirts tucked in, belts straight, buckles polished, hair combed, and shoes shined.

Joey's heart raced during inspection. She was certain the Major could hear her heart pounding as he walked past, but if he could, he ignored it. She did not know if the others felt uneasy, but even if they did, no one would ever admit it.

In the event someone failed inspection, punishment was swift and severe.

"What's this? Corporal Terry Rogers, there's a piece of hair on your uniform."

Joey glanced sideways and saw the major's nose almost touching Terry's. Rogers gulped in horror. This was not the first time she failed inspection. *You'd think she'd learn by now*, Joey thought.

"Step Forward!" He was so close, spit flew from his lips and hit Terry's face.

Terry obeyed without hesitation and did not bother trying to wipe her face. Everyone knew what was coming next. She marched to the front of the room and turned to face the class, her face - beet red.

"Commence!"

Terry began to undress. As she removed each article of clothing, she folded it and placed it on a neat pile on the desk. There was a procedure to follow -- she began with her hat, then her shirt, and kept going until she was completely naked.

"I suggest, Corporal, that you either get your act together and start passing inspection, or you'll find yourself at one of the pleasure farms. Do I make myself clear?"

"Yes, Sir!" Her voice was weak from embarrassment. Joey tried diverting her eyes and tried not to think about the humiliation. Their drill instructors had explained to them what would happen if anyone of them failed inspection. Unfortunately for Terry Rogers, this was not the first time she had experienced this degradation.

Terry anxiously awaited the Major's nod, so she could dress again. Instead, he stood and stared at her. The room was cold, and goose bumps formed on her skin. She could not let herself shiver, or the Major would make things worse for her.

Each minute felt like an eternity to Joey, and she wondered how Terry felt.

Finally, Major Doyle nodded and Terry grabbed quickly for her uniform. "In the proper order!" he barked.

She gulped and placed her uniform back onto the desk, then she began the slow, meticulous formula for redressing and combing her hair.

Joey looked into Terry's eyes and saw that the Major had broken her will.

I will never let him break me like that. Even if it means death, neither he nor anyone else will ever break me down. I won't give him the satisfaction he demonstrates with Rogers.

The expectation was that as Terry dressed, the original problem would be corrected. If not, she would be forced to endure it again until everything was perfect.

During the process, the rest of the class had to stand at attention and watch. If anyone snickered or diverted their attention, they would be next in line for the same punishment.

Joey stood at attention with her eyes focused on a brick in the wall slightly above Terry's head. Everyone had to appear as though they were watching intently. The leaders felt that by watching others pay the penalty, it would deter further infractions of the rules.

"Need I remind you, Corporal, that this will go on your permanent record?"

"Understood, Sir!" Terry finished dressing and this time passed the Major's inspection. She moved back to her place next to her desk.

"Now that everyone has passed uniform inspection, let's move on to checking the desks." Major Doyle went to the first desk. "Private First Class Bobby Matthews, there's a pencil out of place."

"It must've rolled, Sir."

"No excuses! It's out of place, and that is not acceptable. Benson, dump the contents of his desk on the floor and kick them around."

Joey gulped when she heard her name called.

"Yes, Sir!"

She moved quickly to obey. If she did not spread things out sufficiently, her desk would be the next one to be dumped.

Bobby waited, then had to gather up his things and put them back into his desk while the rest of the class continued standing at attention. Failing any part of the morning inspection did not sit well with the members of the class. During break, Bobby and Terry would face further punishment and humiliation at the hands of their classmates for forcing everyone to stand at attention longer than necessary.

The Major encouraged such things. He said this promoted good discipline. Joey felt it simply increased his control over everyone.

Bobby put the finishing touches on his desk, then snapped to attention. "Completed, Sir!"

The Major checked it and approved. "Sit!"

Joey felt relieved to finally be allowed to sit. Her legs were aching -- inspection had lasted over ninety minutes that morning.

"Now we'll begin our recitation," Major Doyle said. "Being a loyal servant of this New Order, I understand it is my responsibility to refrain from all displays of emotion. I accept that responsibility, and should I, at any time, go against this policy, I will do my duty and report to one of my superiors for appropriate discipline."

Joey recited with everyone else. Every day was the same. They got up, had breakfast, injections, inspection, recitation, training, lunch, academics, exercise, supper, study, and bed. The words of the recitation invaded and dominated her thoughts, even when she tried to think of other things. She could hear these words in her sleep. Sometimes she imagined them coming from the walls of her cubicle as she slept.

She searched for a pleasant memory every day to fight against this indoctrination, but each time, it became harder to do. There had to be something in her mind to give her strength, a memory to counteract the brainwashing that slowly consumed more and more control over her mind.

Laughter rose from the clouds of the shadows. Bright sunlight accompanied the giggles.

"So high!"

"That's my little girl," Grandmother shouted from the back door. "She can swing so high! I'll start dinner."

The tire swing soared higher and higher into the air. Feeling the wind blow through her hair gave her a sense of invincibility. She was flying. Grandfather pushed harder.

"Higher, Grandfather! Push me higher!"

Suddenly, a loud knock on the door broke off her laughter. They stopped the swing. She ran to her grandfather's strong arms. They walked together to the house to investigate the knock.

When they entered the living room, they saw two big men in military uniforms with guns in hand. Grandmother sat nearby, crying and rubbing her face. It appeared she'd been struck by one of the men.

"What's the meaning of this?" Grandfather demanded.

One of the men pointed his rifle at Grandfather. "The girl comes with us!"

She clutched her grandfather tighter.

"No. She's not going anywhere with you or anyone else. You have no right to come here, strike my wife and steal my granddaughter. Now, get out of here before I throw you out."

"Don't force me to do something you'll regret, old man." The soldier cocked his gun.

The other man yanked Joey away from her grandfather.

"No! Let me go!" She tried to hold on, but the man was too strong. Kicking, screaming, and squirming, she was dragged out of the house. The second man remained behind - keeping his gun trained on her grandparents.

Slam!

Joey looked around nervously, wondering if anyone noticed her daydreaming. Sweat rolled down her back as she relived the nightmare of the past. She glanced at the Major to see if he noticed her inattention. Inatten-

16

tiveness is dangerous.

He continued slamming books on the desk as part of a lesson. Hoping he would not call on her because she had no idea what topic was being discussed. She took a deep breath and tried to calm down. She needed to pay attention to the discussions, but her mind kept trying to pull away from this hellish existence.

Why can't I focus on good memories? She wondered. *Why must the only one I can recall end so badly?* It felt as if her previous life were drifting further out of mind.

She found herself doing things she never would have considered before. Thoughts of abuse and cruelty to those she grew up with controlled her waking moments. When sleep came, there was no relief. The person she had once been was slipping away, and a cruel, civilized savage was slowly taking her place.

This battle raged within her often. She wondered what she was turning into. She did not understand why life was so complicated. There was no one with whom she could share her confusion. If she did, she would probably be sentenced to the pleasure farm or executed.

The battle within her raged, and her stomach ached. She missed her grandparents and even her parents.

Is there anything left of the life I had before the New Order? She wondered.

CHAPTER 3
UNEXPECTED NEWS

The arrival of spring made the children restless and bored. They had been following the same routine for weeks, and their rigorous training demanded some sort of outlet. Fights became a daily occurrence. This was one outlet acceptable to the leaders and was often encouraged.

Joey felt like an overly saturated sponge. She had been exposed to continued violence in films, demanding training, constant physical tests to determine her worthiness, and abusive situations to prepare her for the future. Each piece was designed to reprogram natural responses and to build up tolerance to pain. Fighting with the others was a small release for some, but Joey was reluctant. Beating up on other members of the youth army did not seem appropriate to her. Joey feared that a fight might possibly reveal something about her that she would rather keep inside. She had mixed feelings about the pointless violence and felt sorry for those who became its subjects. She did her best to remain detached and to stay away from these situations.

Staring out of the barracks window, Joey noticed two birds playing on a tree branch. Somewhere inside the shadows of her mind a little girl laughing and playing mocked her. She could scarcely remember who was that little girl was, yet the ghosts of the past haunted her.

Who is that person? Joey wondered. *How long has it been since I laughed at something?*

She felt fortunate that her six-by-ten cubicle included a window. In the morning, the sun's rays flooded in, brightening the drab, green walls as she woke. The sun seemed like the only gentle thing left in the world, and even it could turn cruel in its season.

Joey glanced around the room. A wooden cot and footlocker made the space seem even smaller. Images of a bright-blue room filled with wonderful things teased her from the shadows..

"Stop!" She said aloud.

She shook her head, trying to shake the memories from her brain. She did not want to relive that terrible first day over again, so she decided that room of her mind must be off limits. Things would never return to the way they were, and its about time she accepted that.

How could they?

"Never!" *I'm different now*, she thought. *I'm a soldier ready to kill on command.*

"Hey, Benson, do you always talk to yourself?" Jesse's voice startled her back to reality. Anxiety filled her at the thought of being caught daydreaming. Warily, she turned to face Jesse.

Would he say anything about her daydreaming? Had he noticed?

"Did you hear the rumors?" Jesse did not wait for a reply. Instead, he gloated over a bit of information he thought that he alone was privy to. Standing at the door to her cubicle with a smirk, he walked in and sat on her cot without permission.

"Who said you could come in?" Joey demanded. "Get off, you're wrinkling the blankets."

"Want to make something of it?" He jumped to his feet, ready to fight.

Joey stared. She debated whether to fight and defend her rank and honor, or if she should ignore his challenge and lose the respect of an insubordinate. The hesitation made Jesse taunt her even more.

"Just what I thought. You're a coward. Why they made you a sergeant and not me, I'll never know. It's not fair." He growled.

"What rumor?" Joey tried to change the subject.

"The rumor that we're going to war."

"Going to war?" The words caught in her throat and nearly choked her before she was able to eventually force them out.

"Yeah. Remember the thing we're training for?"

"Who with?"

"Boy, you are really dumb!"

20

"Watch your defiant mouth!"

Jesse, ignoring the rebuke continued, "Remember the war with the south?" We've already conquered the west, and now our New Order's expanding even further. They need their super soldiers fighting for them. After all, we're superior forces." The thought of fighting and inflicting pain on others filled him with eagerness and anticipation.

"When do we find out for sure?"

"I know, but I won't tell you." Jesse sauntered off with a smirk on his face.

"You don't know crap! That's why you're not telling me."

Jesse ignored her.

"If you knew, you'd be bragging about it!" She watched him disappear into his cubicle.

I should march over there and order him to tell me what he knows. She paused. *I don't want to know that badly.*

War, she thought. Her stomach lurched. She moved back to the window. *Why do we have to go to war? Can't we be satisfied pretending to be fighting a war in our training? No one winds up dead that way.*

Only one year earlier, Joey was reading about wars in history class and hearing reports on the news of far off countries bombing each other. Soon, she would be fighting one of her own. Joey's mind filled with fear, thinking of what could happen during a war. Graphic pictures filled her mind, scenes from the training movies they were forced to watch repeatedly. The leaders especially enjoyed watching vivid displays of blood and dismembered bodies. The purpose was to steel them against these horrors, so they could go on and do their duty. Joey felt sick as her mind ran wild with those horrible images.

"Attention on deck!" a voice called.

Leaving her thoughts and questions behind, Joey hurried to the opening of her cubicle and snapped to attention. Major Doyle entered the room a moment later.

"I have information that concerns you." He paced up and down the center aisle, looking from side to side at the young warriors sizing them up as he passed by.

"The young people's militia of this sector has proven its worthiness to serve the New Order in its current endeavors. Now you'll be given an even greater opportunity to render aid," he beamed with pride. "Therefore, we have decided to reward your loyalty. In two days, you'll be moved to another camp where your training can be intensified.

Intensified? How much more intense can we get?

"After six weeks at this camp, you'll take your place at one of the frontline camps along the southeastern border. There, you'll step forward to expand our New Order. You will make us all proud."

He moved toward the doorway, then stopped. "One more thing. In light of this mission, the leaders have determined it would be in the best interest of the New Order to allow your relatives a brief visit. We feel this is good public relations. Rest assured, we do not need good public relations. It is not good to fight a war on two fronts. We feel that this visit will quench the rumors the Resistance Movement is stirring up. During the visit, your relatives will be assured of your health and welfare and your superiority to go to war. As you were!"

The young people lifted an expected cheer for their found favor.

Talk of a visit, the Resistance, and the impeding war all worked together to make Joey's stomach dance around. She had not seen any of her relatives since the night they had been paraded onto the platform, and Jesse's uncle died. The shock on everyone's face was still etched into her memory.

As for the Resistance, she was undecided about it. She knew the leaders hated it, yet many well-respected people were rumored to accept its principles. Some were actively involved searching for ways to overthrow the Militia. Yet, association with anyone connected with the movement was considered treason.

Rumors even stated that some top officials might be involved. The Resistance tried to infiltrate every position in the New Order with the hope of regaining control of the government and allowing people to once again travel. Anyone might be a member. Joey shook her head and determined to ignore these thoughts and try to focus on the impending visit.

Who would come? If I'm lucky, no one. That would be just fine, because I wouldn't know what to say to them. I don't want them to see me this way.

She wondered how to handle the visit, then she remembered her grandparents' faces before that dreadful day.

She felt bright sunlight and the wind in her hair. There was a loud knock at the door. . . .

"No! No more!"

"Who are you talking to, Sarge?" Randy asked.

Terror nearly overwhelmed her. "Just thinking out loud." She tried to sound assured.

Randy walked on.

Joey sighed. That was too close. She had to guard her thoughts more carefully. If that had been Major Doyle, the consequences would have been severe.

The days crawled by, even though the pace of their activities had increased. There was packing to do and weapons to be prepared.

After an eternity, the day of the visit arrived. Joey was uncertain which she dreaded more, the impending visit or the life-and-death conflict facing her.

The young warriors were assembled outside the great hall. Two guards escorted the relatives into the room and assigned them to tables. Fear and anticipation shown on their faces as they awaited the children's arrival.

"Attention!" the guard ordered. "March proudly. You're the New Order's finest," he beamed.

Another guard led them into the hall. Each compatriot marched with mechanical precision as the group entered the room. Joey held her breath as she marched past her grandparents' table.

As soon as Jane and Henry Benson saw Joey, their expressions changed to relief. Grandfather was so overjoyed that he jumped up and moved quickly toward Joey, who marked time in the ranks. The guard quickly grabbed him and shoved him roughly back to the table with the butt of his rifle.

"Sit down, or you'll be escorted out," he barked.

"Halt!" another guard ordered the children.

They stopped in unison.

"Fall out!"

Each one moved slowly to their assigned tables. Mother, grandparents, aunts, and others eagerly waited for the chance to spend a few minutes with their flesh and blood.

Joey examined her grandparents' face as she slowly approached the table. They seemed to have aged a lot since that first day. She wondered if that came from the changes in the New Order or from concern about her.

Why would they worry about me?

When she came near the table, her grandfather jumped to his feet again to hug her. She recoiled, fearing anyone touching her, and automatically assumed a fighting stance. The brainwashing had penetrated her deepest emotions. It had control of her whether she wanted to admit it or not. Suddenly Grandfather was considered the enemy.

Henry's expression became sadder as he watched his granddaughter, standing there waiting to attack him, possibly even kill him with one wrong move.

"Henry, come sit down." Jane tried to diffuse the situation. She was a small, middle-aged woman with an indomitable spirit. Since the Militia removed Joey from their home, Jane Benson had become very compliant. She tried not to stir up trouble. Her spunk seemed to have drifted away. "You don't want them to end the visit before it starts."

He moved slowly back to the table and sat down. Joey relaxed her stance and moved forward cautiously, sitting across from them. They stared at each other in silence.

"How are you, Joey?" Henry asked, trying to start a conversation.

"I'm functioning well." She looked into her grandmother's eyes, which were red. She wondered if grandmother had been crying recently.

Why would she cry? Is there something wrong? If so, why would one cry? How would crying help? Crying doesn't change reality.

The moments of silence were awkward for everyone. Glancing at her compatriots at nearby tables, she noticed they, too, seemed uncomfortable and unable to communicate to their relatives.

Why had the New Order insisted on this?

"How's mother and father?" Joey asked trying to break the silence. It was odd that those were the words exiting her mouth. Joey had not had much contact with her parents since she was born.

"They wanted to come, but they couldn't bear to see you here, knowing that you couldn't come home with us," Jane answered awkwardly.

"I see." Her face showed skepticism.

Since when did Mother and Father care if I came home or not.

"Is there anything you need?" Henry asked.

"I'm told I have all that I need."

"I see." Anger flashed in his eyes. He bit his lip to stop his anger from exploding.

"It was good of you to come," Joey changed the subject before he had another outburst. She wanted them to know she still thought about them. It seemed important to them.

"It was good of you to see us." They chimed.

"Have they told you we're leaving for a while?"

"Yes. Do you want to go?" Grandfather inquired.

"That's not open to discussion," Joey snapped.

What an odd question? What did it matter if I wanted to go or not? I received orders to go and go I must? Why would he ask such a question?

"What if I told you I could arrange it so you don't need to go?" Henry leaned over the table to whisper to her.

Joey backed away. "That's not an option. I'm not allowed to discuss such matters with you. It's sufficient that I must go to serve the New Order. You must understand that! Anything else is treason."

Joey's eyes darted around the room. She was afraid that someone may have overheard Grandfather's words. Or worse, had been listening.

"Of course," Jane said trying to sound understanding.

"Please be careful out there," Henry said. "Despite what they've done to you, you're still our little girl....We love you."

Joey looked away. A sudden ache in her throat made it difficult to talk.

What was it about those words that make my throat ache? What do they mean, "love"? They do not know me anymore, they cannot love me.

25

"Visitation is over," the guard announced.

"Will you come again?" Joey asked.

"Any time they allow us," Henry answered. "What I'm about to say may not make sense to you now, but please try to remember it....Don't lose the little girl inside you." He stood taking grandmother in his arm.

Joey stared in confusion.

What does that mean? He's right, it doesn't make sense.

"Fall in!" The order rang throughout the room.

Joey hustled to get into line before she was punished for dawdling.

Jane and Henry watched her march across the room with the other miniature soldiers - their childhood innocence stolen from them. They were no longer children but soldier-like robots. They were becoming civilized savages. They watched as long as they could, but in a flash, the last of the children disappeared.

Joey watched from her window as her grandparents walked out of the compound and down the road toward home, two miles away. Her eyes followed them until they rounded a curve and disappeared.

With the promise of being sent to war, Joey wondered , *Will that be the last I see of them?*

CHAPTER 4
WHAT MAKES A GOOD SOLDIER?

Once the last of the families left the compound, the children were marched over to the supply depot to receive the equipment they would need. As Joey picked up her high-powered laser rifle, pistol, map, compass, helmet, flak jacket, and hunting knife; reality began to overwhelm Joey as if she were hit by a truck.

The young soldiers were divided into teams of approximately six each. The team selections were designed so that their skills would complement each other. As each patrol stood waiting for orders, Major Doyle approached Joey's group first.

"Sergeant Benson, due to your outstanding performance to date, I have placed you in command of this patrol."

"Thank you, Sir!" Joey beamed.

Leadership roles were coveted positions. This translated to favors and acceptance. Members of the youth army would literally kill each other, if it meant that they would get a promotion.

What makes me stand out? I'm nothing special. If they could read my thoughts, command would not be what they'd offer me.

Joey studied each member of her team, mentally noting the skills that made them valuable or unique. The right combination of skills makes an effective team. The wrong combination could be deadly.

Corporal Jesse Burrows was twelve, enthusiastic, overzealous and often cruel. He enjoyed fighting and loved inflicting pain on others. He was anxious to have his own command and would do anything to get it. He was a definite threat to her leadership. Caution was warranted.

I'll need to watch my back with him on my team.

Next was Corporal Terry Rogers, age ten. Joey could not imagine how Terry made it this far, but not only was she still in the program, she was in an elite group. Terry was less aggressive than most and was often in trouble. She became ill during the movies and often failed inspection. Joey had not figured out Terry's unique skill. Knowing Terry could be kicked out of the program at any time, Joey wanted to limit her responsibility. Joey did not want anything to happen during her command. Perhaps, the present situation might give Terry the opportunity to succeed.

Privates First Class Randy and Bobby Matthews were twins. The only way to tell them apart was how they parted their hair. Although they were only ten years old, they had sharper skills than many of their trainers. Their cunningness had been exhibited many times during their training.

Last was Private Charlie Jones, age ten. She was small but supposedly made up for her size in other ways. Joey wondered how she would fare under fire. Charlie was in a different class at the academy, so Joey did not know much about her. She would have a chance to observe Charlie and, possibly, give an evaluation of her during the coming exercises. That would be a good sign -- only those favored by the leaders were asked to give evaluations.

During the preparations for the mission, Grandfather's words continued to haunt her. She could not imagine why they still loved her.

They don't even know me anymore. No one should love me. Love makes you weak, and I can't afford to be weak. They saw me stand there and let Jason Burrows die.

Open-backed trucks lined the driveway of the compound, waiting to carry the young warriors to six weeks of intense combat training. Those weeks promised to be more brutal than experienced previously. A feeling of excitement filled the air. The children were anxious to test their skills and have a break in their routine. Their programming encouraged them to look forward to war.

Team members waited around the trucks, passing the time by discussing the gains made in the battles. It was a safe subject as long as one did not discuss any moral implications.

"Fall in!" Joey ordered, surprised at the fierceness in her voice.

The five members of her patrol lined up with their packs, heavy with the equipment they would need for the coming weeks. Besides their packs the team had rifles hanging from their shoulders, knives and pistols strapped to their belts, and compasses stowed in their pockets. Without the weapons, they would have looked like a group of Scouts preparing for a field trip.

The patrols boarded the trucks in an orderly fashion, and each patrol sat together. The ride to the training camp would take more than two hours.

Sitting next the railing, Joey refused to make small talk about the battles with her seat mate, Charlie. Instead, Joey focused her attention on the passing scenery. Imagining the trees waving *bon voyages,* she managed to shut out the buzz of conversation around her. The hum of the truck's engine gave her a strange feeling of tranquility.

As they rode through the different neighborhoods, Joey saw swing sets and sand boxes -- all deserted. There were no children in any of the backyards they passed. Every child was the property of the Militia. The New Order refused to share its resource with anyone, including their parents.

They arrived at camp in time for lunch. Each person exited the truck and lined up for their meal. The field camp did not have automated food dispensers like those at the academy. Instead, there were soldiers handing out scoops of food. Everyone would eat the same thing in the same quantity, quite different from the special diets given them at their homebase.

During lunch, the children were informed that a round of war games would start immediately after they stowed their gear. The games would determine each teams' weaknesses and need for further instruction.

After lunch, they were led to a large barracks that would become their home for a while. It was a long, drab building with bunk beds lining both walls. Each set of beds was separated by small footlockers where their gear would be stored. It was very different from the private cubicles they had at their home base.

Joey stood at the end of the building and stared. She missed the cozy feeling of her cubicle. The openness of her new "home" made her feel vulnerable. There would be no room for lapses in memory or daydreaming.

Setting her anxious feelings aside, she began to mentally prepare for the war games.

The teams were divided into the red and the blue armies. Joey's team was assigned to the blue army. At the designated hour, she led her team to the assigned coordinates. They took up a position at the entrance of a large wooded area to wait for the games to begin. She hoped her patrol would make a good showing. The team's orders were to prevent the red army from entering the forest. If the red army managed to do that, they would win the games.

Everyone was issued a special rifle and handgun that shot blue dye. Each team was given grenades which were small balloon-like objects filled with dye. The dye would let the officials know who to count as casualties during the mock-battle.

"Rogers and Matthews, B., hide in these bushes," Joey ordered. "Jones and Burrows, branch off and scout to the right. Matthews, R, come with me, we'll take the left side."

The team members saluted and moved into position.

As Joey and Randy walked cautiously beside the woods, they heard voices. Scurrying into the underbrush, they lay on their bellies and saw three red army members standing in front of them.

"What do you think the blue army plans to do?"

"Don't know. They're a tricky bunch."

"They're probably nearby."

"Yeah, I'd think they'd have some guys guarding the woods."

Joey thought about the instructions concerning prisoners of war. To be taken prisoner during the games promised to be extremely humiliating. Such soldiers were stripped to their underwear, then hogtied and left in the woods near the place of their capture. The thought of being captured sent a shiver up her spine.

At the end of the games, all the POWs would be marched through the camp and ridiculed. Afterward, the winning army would reclaim its people.

Those would be allowed to dress, but the capture would be written into their records.

But that would only be the beginning for the losing army's captives. The entire losing army would be rounded up and marched onto the parade grounds for punishment.

Joey and Randy hid in the bushes and waited.

Should we attack or wait? That was the question that plagued her. This would not be a time to start second guessing herself. While she was still thinking about her course of action, Randy suddenly sneezed. She motioned to Randy to save their grenades for later. Randy followed her lead as they attacked the group in hand-to-hand fashion. They had to be careful in case more of the red army was nearby. Their main objective was to prevent this patrol from sending a warning signal to other members of the red army.

The three members of the red army patrol spun and reached for their weapons. Joey and Randy leaped on them before they could use their guns or sound a warning whistle. Three against two were not bad odds in a fist fight, but the red army scouts tried to change the odds by grabbing sticks and swinging them viciously at Randy and Joey. All is considered fair. The games had few rules -- almost anything was allowed.

Joey dodged a stick as it hurled passed her head. Another swing caught her leg and sent her sprawling to the ground. Ignoring the pain, she rolled out of the way as a scout dived at her. She got to her feet and quickly wrestled him to the ground and hogtied him.

Before long, she and Randy subdued the remaining two. Once all three scouts were bound and gagged, Joey and Randy sat down to catch their breath.

Joey wondered if her guards were still alert under the bushes. Her mind jumped to her other scouting team, she prayed they would show some savvy. Failure by any member of the team would look bad for her.

Once Joey was convinced no one else was coming, she moved her prisoners farther into the bushes. Randy used his knife to cut off the prisoners' uniforms. Joey slit their red arm bands and stuffed them in her pocket so she could prove they captured them.

As Joey and Randy turned to go, they kicked the prisoners a few times to give them something extra to think about while waiting for the end of the games.

Joey was glad the red patrol had not been victorious. The prisoners could possibly lay there all day before being released. Often times the POWs were hidden to avoid detection by their comrades. Depending on how well the prisoners were hidden, it could be hours and even days before these prisoners were found. The whole idea of that would drive her crazy.

Joey returned to the entrance to the woods and found Terry and Bobby alert and hiding in the bushes. Jesse and Charlie returned moments later. Each group gave their reports. Joey's had been the only capture for the team. No one else even sighted the enemy. Joey gathered her troops and made plans for their next move.

Distant shouts caught her attention. She wondered if it was the red army in retreat. Joey waited for her team to take up positions behind nearby trees. The core of the blue army had outmaneuvered the red army and was chasing them toward the woods. The red army was retreating. Joey's patrol waited with weapons ready.

When the red army came within range, Joey's group started firing. Grenades flew striking several members of the retreating army and soaking them with dye. Between the accuracy of the grenades and the marksmanship of the rifle fire, the red army was prevented from entering the forest. The blue army surrounded them. There was nothing left but for the red army to surrender in humiliating defeat.

That round of the war games was over. The blue army had one win under their belts.

Joey felt tired but happy. Her patrol was instrumental in the victory. They might earn a commendation. She stood and watched as guards rounded up the captured members of the red army and marched them around the parade ground. The blue army waited to abuse them.

She had done well in command. Her tactics were correct. She led her troops into battle, captured prisoners, and was a valuable asset in the red army's final defeat.

Wow, she thought. *I'm really good at this.*

The blue army marched back to the training camp, leaving the red army in custody of the leaders for further training and punishment. Their victory guaranteed them a prominent place when they were shipped to the front. For the moment, they could revel in their victory. Members of the blue army received the rest of the day off and extra rations for dinner.

The only thing I want is to get more acquainted with my bed.

The past few days had been stressful. Joey lay on her cot and tried to relax, hoping for sleep to come. Her mind wandered, but this time there were no memories of a little girl with a ponytail fighting to the surface, only thoughts of soldiers killing and abusing their enemies.

As she drifted off to sleep, images from the day's game replayed in her mind.

The next morning, training resumed for everyone. The previous day's glory was a distant memory. When reveille sounded at 0500, everyone stood on equal ground again.

Today's activities included a timed run through the obstacle course.

Joey led her troops to the obstacle course. They would be the third group to run. She watched the first two groups run the course. Each had practiced the course dozens of times at their home base. This one seemed similar, but worse in that it was considerably more difficult. Many of her peers failed the course at one point or another. These failures of course brought severe consequences.

"Benson," the Captain called, "your patrol's next."

"Yes, sir!"

"You'll be the first one from your group. It'll be your responsibility to show them how it's done."

"Yes, Sir!"

A twinge of fear crept in as she thought about that. *What if I fail?* She wondered. *What if I'm a bad example? That would be worse than if one of them fails.*

She took a deep breath, and clenched her jaw hoping to stop all the what ifs.

"Go!" the Captain shouted.

Joey ran so fast her feet barely touched the ground. Wind blew in her face, giving her a sense of freedom, but that vanished as she approached the first obstacle -- barbed wire. She tried to visualize the right moment to throw herself to the ground and begin the crawl under the wire without losing time or momentum. Too early or too late would be very costly.

She threw herself to the ground and landed hard on her belly. The impact jarred her bones and sprayed sand into her mouth, but her timing was perfect. Crawling through dirt and mud, she slithered the next ten yards in good time.

Pausing only long enough to wipe mud from her eyes, she sprang to her feet, jumped over the pommel horse, and continued with a leap into the air. Her outstretched hand grabbed the overhead bar and swung her feet up to a ledge. Leaping over the fence and onto a jungle gym, she swung to the ground and continued on the long run. Jumping onto one end of the bobbing log, she carefully scampered across the twelve feet to the other side.

So far, so good, she thought. *Careful Benson, overconfidence will slow you down.*

She leaped head first through the suspended tire, somersalted, rolled to her feet and hurried on. Up ahead were the log hurdles, the hand-over-hand wall climb, the rope climbs, a swing across the puddle, and three laps around the track. Joey took each challenge in turn with only a couple of stumbles along the way, she managed to recover without losing time.

At the finish line, she felt relief when everyone's attention now focused on another.

"Not bad, Benson," the Captain said.

Breathing heavily, Joey forced herself to stand up straight and take deep breaths as she watched her team mates heading toward the finish line.

As each trainee took his turn, others scrutinized their performances. There were no shouts of encouragement, only stony silence. Each soldier wanted to out perform their compatriots.

Next came the relay race. Each patrol would compete against the others. Joey lined up her people in the order she thought best. They had to carry rifles in their hands and empty ammunition magazines in their teeth. Joey was pleased, it was a difficult run, but her team performed well.

The next event on the training schedule was battling with pugil sticks. She was paired off against Jesse. Each wore helmets with protective face guards, mouth guards, and gloves. The four-foot pugil sticks had hard rubber cushions on either end.

She and Jesse were called into the middle of the circle.

"Go!" the guard said.

Joey smashed at Jesse with repeated blows from her stick. Jesse returned each blow as forcefully as he received it. Each must stay close enough to the other so they would not be disqualified for stepping outside of the circle. After a long time, Jesse began a flurry of blows that ended with him sweeping her feet out from under her.

"You cheated!" Joey ripped off her helmet.

"There are no rules in combat." Jesse replied.

Joey's pride was hurt, but she could not show it.

Last came target practice. Joey led the patrol to the barracks to retrieve their rifles, then they went to the firing range. Each person picked a target and started firing.

"Hey, Sergeant," Charlie called.

"What?"

"My gun's having problems."

Joey turned and saw Charlie pointing the gun directly toward her. In panic, Joey grabbed the barrel and shoved downward. The surprised Charlie jumped and pulled the trigger. Bullets flew in all directions while Charlie danced around in fear. She struck two tires on the Captain's jeep and put a hole in the water supply for the day. Joey finally wrestled the gun away and the barrage of bullets ceased.

"Jones, you'll be punished for your stupidity and carelessness!" She was aware that the Captain was watching.

"I'm sorry."

"Sorry doesn't cut it." Joey growled.

During the march back to the barracks, Charlie was forced to run circles around the rest of the patrol with her weapon held overhead. She stumbled and fell many times. Each time, Joey shouted, grabbed her collar, and yanked her to her feet.

"Keep moving!" she said.

"Will she make it back? Randy asked.

"She'll probably drop dead." Jesse laughed. "It's been a while since I saw a dead body up close. When was your last time?"

Randy eyed Jesse in disbelief.

Charlie dragged herself into the barracks. Joey sat on her bunk and watched Charlie straggle in, followed by Major Doyle. He carried a large wooden paddle with holes in it.

Charlie was forced to remove her pants and underwear before bending over to hold onto the lower bunk's frame. Major Doyle spanked her with the paddle, and the crack of wood hitting Charlie's bare bottom made Joey's stomach cringe.

Charlie never made a sound. It would've been worse if she had. When the Major finished, she had large red welts on her butt. She dressed carefully and lay on her bunk on her stomach.

Joey felt confused by conflicting feelings -- compassion for Charlie and the desire to punish her for being so stupid.

Why do I feel like this? Joey wondered. *Why was Charlie so stupid? Doesn't she know she almost killed people today? Why is all this punishment necessary? Can't we go home and resume our lives as children?*

For the entire six weeks, Joey led her patrol in various exercises -- the obstacle course, long runs with full packs, war games, and target practice. The six weeks passed. Sometimes, time dragged from the training and constant abuse. At other times, it moved all too quickly.

Soon, they were ready to depart for the battle. Joey knew they would face real combat, fighting where people will die or others would be permanently mutilated.

They got orders to depart for the front lines, then they boarded the trucks and were transported into the combat zone. The Militia's super-soldiers, a superior race of fighting machines composed of ten- to seventeen-year-olds, were entering a real battle zone. These super-soldiers would test their training, special diets, and the chemicals to prove whether or not the New Order's way was the right way.

Joey groped for some memory of the little girl her grandfather asked her to remember, but brainwashing of the present was much too strong. Her failure to find such memories bothered her. She had been that little girl longer than she had been a soldier, but she could not remember anything about her.

Perhaps, as the Major said, "It's all in the making of a good soldier."

CHAPTER 5
EXPANSION AT WHAT PRICE?

Joey and her team arrived at the bunker. It was a ten-by-twenty structure made of reinforced concrete and sandbags. The main access was through a heavy wooden door that was partly below ground.

Once inside, they were greeted by a dark, dreary, dank room. As Joey surveyed the room, she noticed a table with a two-way radio and six small cots that were the scant furnishings. All of the intense training and preparation had not prepared her for the dismal reality of a combat-zone bunker. The dampness inside the structure sent shivers down her spine.

She took a one last breath of fresh air and walked into the bunker. "Welcome to your new home." She tried to sound upbeat.

The others stared at her, unable to appreciate her attempt at being positive.

"Pick a spot for the duration," she ordered.

Each moved a cot to a section of the floor and used his belongings to stake out his territory. They scarcely began to unpack when a rocket barrage came.

"Stay in your bunkers!" a gruff voice shouted over the radio.

"Get your helmets on!" Joey commanded, amazed she was able to think of something practical at such a time.

"Looks like they're throwing a welcome-to-the-area party," the voice on the radio added.

Flashes of light came through the cracks around the door, reminding Joey of fireworks she had seen in a previous life. A rocket landed so close to the bunker that it jarred her back to reality. The next one rattled her teeth.

Shaking with fear, Joey tried not to show her panic. As the leader, she had to set an example. The best way to ease her fear was to focus her mind on her troops. She needed to be sure they were battle ready. Their reaction to all of this might mean life or death to the rest of the group.

She crawled over to Terry and was shocked to find her crying silently. "What are you doing?" she whispered angrily. "What if someone else saw you?....I should report you.... Don't be such a baby! Pull yourself together!"

"I'm sorry, but I'm scared!" Terry whined.

"You'd better get a hold of yourself before anyone else sees you. If the others see you like this, I'll be forced to report you and you will be finished. There's a certain amount of fear in all of us, but how you deal with that fear makes you a superior soldier and compliance means survival."

She noticed a wet spot on Terry's pants. She flew into a rage. "What did you do that for?"

"I'm sorry. When the rockets started, I....I lost control."

Fighting for control, Joey spoke in a calmer voice, "Change your pants and get it together. Forget we had this conversation, or we're both finished." Joey shook her head in disgust and crawled over to Jesse.

"Isn't this great?" Jesse was like a kid at a carnival. "Let's go out there and get in the middle of it!" He started to get up.

Joey grabbed his belt and yanked him back to the floor. "Stay put."

"I want some action."

"I'm in charge. You stay here until I say otherwise. Is that clear?"

"Yeah, sure. Why'd we come to this wasteland if all we're going to do is sit in a bunker when the action's outside?" Jesse complained.

"We'll see plenty of action soon."

"Right!" Jesse started to get up again.

"Burrows, you will sit down and shut up and that's an order!" Joey growled.

Joey was not certain what Jesse had in mind, but with her in charge, he had to obey or suffer the consequences. Youth officers were targeted by their peers seeking to advance to command. Jesse was one who would do it any way he could. He wanted to control others. If he had found Terry, she would have been done for. He was merciless.

Jesse sat with his back to the wall, tearing up pieces of paper, and throw-

40

ing them to the floor with a look that showed he was scheming.

Joey crawled over to the twins and found them in good spirits.

"I can't wait until it's our turn," Bobby said.

"How soon before we get into the action?" Randy asked.

"I don't know. The Major will give us orders shortly."

Joey went to Charlie, who did not speak. She sat on the floor with her knees drawn to her chest and rocked back and forth. Joey shook her head and went back to her cot to wait.

Explosions kept rocking the bunker.

What if we die during this attack? Joey mused. *Maybe that would be best. At least this nightmare would be over.*

After twenty minutes, the attack ended as abruptly as it began.

"All clear," the radio announced.

"Let's go out to check the damage," Joey said. "Jones, carry the radio. It is essential to stay in touch with the command post. Charlie picked up the radio and fell into pace at the end of the line."

Walking outside, they nearly stumbled into an enormous crater beside the bunker. Another foot and that rocket could have killed them.

As she lifted her foot to step forward, Joey pulled it back and mentally cringed. Her stomach churned as she saw the body of one of the children. Somehow all their training films did not prepare her for the real thing. She looked at his youthful face. He probably was about the same age as she was. She wondered why he had to die so senselessly. With a swallow, she tried to get her stomach under control.

She closed her eyes and stepped over the body. Terry and Charlie muffled gags as they walked past the body. Her throat tightened, and she took a deep breath, hoping not to vomit.

Control! Must retain control!

After a brief tour of the area to survey the damage, the patrol joined the others in the assembly hall. The team members milled around with the others.

Major Doyle called all patrol leaders to a strategy meeting. He began by assigning the groups various duties.

Joey wondered what her group would be stuck with. She hoped it was something safe, like guarding the camp. She waited nervously as the Major called off name after name and explained their assignment.

"Benson," the Major said, "you and your people will be on reconnaissance."

Reconnaissance! Her heart almost jumped to her throat. This meant she would have to lead her patrol deep into enemy territory and scout the enemy's strengths and weaknesses, but they were not allowed to engage the enemy. But that is not saying the enemy would not try to engage them. It also meant that there was the risk that any one of them could be injured, killed, or captured. None of the options were appealing.

Feelings of inadequacy nearly consumed her. During all the war games, they practiced offensive and defensive tactics. The one area their trainers did not spend much time on was reconnaissance. It seemed she would have to invent her tactics as they went along.

The meeting ended and Joey returned to her patrol. "Fall in!"

The five members scurried back to the bunker to get their packs and get into a line in front of it.

"Attention!"

Everyone snapped to attention. Joey studied their faces. The oldest of the group was only twelve years old. She was about to put all of them into a situation that children should never be called upon to face. Some of them might end up dead.

"Listen up. We've been assigned to reconnaissance. We leave within the hour. You'll report to supply and get additional ammunition, food, and then go to the infirmary and pickup your vitamin supplement. We'll be away from camp for a while. That's all. Dismissed!"

The hour passed quickly. She would be leading her troops into danger. She gave each member a position to walk. As they left, the group looked like a diamond. Joey led the way on the point position. On her right side were the twins. Terry and Jesse were on the left. Charlie, with the radio, came at the rear.

"Keep your eyes open for anything out of the ordinary." Joey ordered.

Wandering through the woods, Joey stared at the trees, looking for signs of movement. The last thing she wanted was to meet would be an enemy soldier face-to-face. Trees waved branches like sinister claws in the air. She wondered if they would grab her before the enemy did.

The ground was soft as they hiked through the woods. It felt like walking on sponges. A gray squirrel scampered from tree to tree, keeping pace with them. It was almost welcome company.

"I don't feel right about this war," Randy whispered.

"I don't imagine anyone feels right about a war," she replied and motioned for Randy to keep quiet.

They reached a clearing overlooking a lake. The shimmering water nearly blinded Joey. She ducked behind a tree to avoid the bright sunlight and wondered if any enemy patrols were nearby. She heard ducks calling in their unique cadence as they flew overhead. Suddenly, the rhythm of the wildlife was interrupted by machine-gun fire.

"Hit the deck!" Joey shouted.

All six children lay on their bellies while Joey tried to determine where the gunfire came from. "Burrows."

"Yeah?"

"Thanks for volunteering." It seemed only right to send the guy that was anxious to get himself into the fighting. "I want you to crawl over to that clearing and see if you can tell where that machine gun is. Come back to report so we can map it."

"Can't we blow it up?"

"No. If we try to take out that machine-gun nest we'll be signaling to every enemy soldier within miles of our position. Our job is to map, not blow up."

Jesse made a disgusted face, but nodded his obedience. He dodged from tree to tree, reminding Joey of the squirrel they had seen earlier. The machine gunner saw Jesse and fired at him.

"Rogers, cover him," Joey said.

Terry took a position behind a tree and fired toward the machine-gun nest.

As Jesse came closer to the clearing, he dropped to his belly and started crawling. Instead of stopping where he had been ordered to, Jesse kept moving. Suddenly, he lobbed a grenade. Joey presumed it was in the nest. A loud explosion followed, then silence.

Jesse trotted back with a smile on his face.

"What did you think you were doing?" Joey demanded.

"I saw the situation and adapted to the need." He replied glibly.

"You disobeyed a direct order, Mister."

"I did not! I improvised. We already announced our presence here by returning fire. I just made sure that gun would not trouble anyone else."

"Consider yourself on report." Joey turned to direct her remarks to the others. "Now..."

"Wait a minute!" He stepped in front of her. "Why should I be on report, when I saved our lives?"

"What do you want, a medal? Look, the bottom line is, you disobeyed a direct order, and the New Order doesn't look on that very highly. Now, get out of my way!"

Jesse shoved her, and she shoved back.

"You're digging yourself into a hole!"

Jesse turned to walk away, but he spun around and punched Joey in the mouth. The others grabbed him, before he could get off another sucker punch.

"You just sealed your coffin." Joey picked herself up and rubbed her jaw. "Let's get out of here before someone comes to check on their comrades. I'll take care of your later, Burrows."

Joey was disgusted with herself for allowing her guard to be lowered enough for Jesse to get that punch in.

The patrol walked past the area of the destroyed machine-gun nest. Joey noticed the dead were not any older than herself. She took a deep breath and kept going. Smoke rose among the twisted, mutilated bodies of the enemy. The sight of brains mixed with intestines made her stomach churn.

They walked deeper into the woods. She tried vainly to put the sight from her mind.

The movies are not quite the same, even when the scenes are the same.

After a couple of weeks, the patrol returned to camp, dirty and hungry. Before they could catch a bite to eat or get cleaned up, Major Doyle ordered them to his tent.

They walked in and snapped to attention with a salute.

"Report," the Major said.

Joey stepped forward and pulled out the map she made of their travels. Major Doyle studied it, pacing in front of the young warriors.

Joey shifted her weight and hoped the Major had not noticed her nervousness.

"Explain these symbols, Benson," the Major commanded.

"The squares are known enemy positions. Most have only a few soldiers. The one with the red X was destroyed."

"Destroyed?"

"Yes, Sir."

"Your orders were for reconnaissance. You were to avoid combat at all costs, correct?"

"Yes sir."

"Then explain this."

"I ordered Corporal Burrows to check a machine-gun nest we had found. He moved in closer than necessary, and on his own volition, destroyed the nest with a grenade. That action was in direct violation of the orders I gave."

"Burrows, is that true?"

Jesse stepped forward and said, "Yes, Sir!"

"I like a soldier with some initiative," Major beamed.

Joey was not sure why she did not tell the Major about Jesse's assault on her.

Jesse's eyes glowed with pride and satisfaction, while Joey's burned with anger.

"However, obeying orders is important in a chain of command. Your actions announced our presence to the enemy. Discipline breaks down when soldiers do not follow orders. Orders save lives! It may have been Sergeant Benson had a good reason for the order and did not feel the need to explain it to you. Do you have anything to say for yourself?"

There was no response to the Major's question.

Jesse's glow of pride changed to anger, but he held his tongue.

"I didn't think you would. I sentence you to three days of disciplinary action. The choice of discipline will be up to your commanding officer. You

45

are to obey every order Sergeant Benson gives you without question. Is that clear?"

"Yes, Sir!" Jesse became even more angry.

"One more thing, Burrows. It had better not happen again." The Major's expression was stern. "Get yourself cleaned up and get some chow. Take twenty-four hours to rest. After which, Sergeant, you will carry out Burrows' discipline. The rest of you will observe his punishment and learn from it. Dismissed."

Each of them saluted, did an about face, and marched out. Once outside, they scattered in order to be alone. They wanted to be anywhere other than with the group they had spent the past couple of weeks with. After spending all that time scouting together, they were sick of being a group.

Joey wandered toward the bunker. When she heard someone running up behind her, she whirled. It was Jesse.

He stopped a short distance away. "You'd better watch your back. I'll get even with you for putting a blotch on my record. You could've over-looked this little matter out in the field. We accomplished our mission. What difference did it make how we did it? The end justified the means."

"The Major questioned the map markings, and I followed his orders. Just be glad I didn't mention that you struck your commanding officer." She managed to suppress her fear of him. "You better watch your threats mister, or the blotch on your record will be the least of your worries."

Jesse walked away without a response.

Joey knew she had a formidable enemy in Jesse. Caution was the order of the day around him. She would still need to make his punishment as de-manding as if he were anyone else.

No one will be able to accuse me of being unfair.

When she got back to the bunker, Joey stretched out on her small cot. Her muscles ached with weariness. As she tried to relax, she forced her mind to try and think of a pleasant memory, anyone would do, but her mind kept replaying scenes from the past few weeks. The only pictures her mind could see were the mutilated bodies of the enemy.

She survived her first mission, but at what price? She had further created a formidable enemy, vivid pictures etched in her mind, and reinforced all of the Militia's programming. Her mind was filled with horror. She wondered if she would ever be able to close her eyes again and not see the ugliness.

Twenty-four hours passed quicker than she would have liked. Time for Jesse to be disciplined. He reported to Joey in the center of camp. Anyone who wanted to watch was welcome. The members of Joey's patrol were required to be there and taunt Jesse, as humiliation was a part of his punishment. All of this would make Jesse even more dangerous to Joey.

The first thing she had him do was run in a tight circle while raising his rifle from his waist to overhead and back. To make it harder, Joey threw buckets of water in his face.

"A little wet, Burrows?" Bobby jeered.

The others laughed.

"You won't need a shower tonight," Randy added.

After a while, Jesse tired and stumbled.

"Poor baby," Terry said. "He's tired."

The team members enjoyed Jesse's discipline more than others.

Next, Joey had Jesse do one hundred pushups in the mud created by the water.

"Get your face in the puddle," she ordered.

With a grimace, Jesse obeyed. On the drop, his face went into the mud.

"How does that taste?" Charlie taunted. "A little mud soup?"

"Getting tired, Burrows?" Randy asked. "I'm not. Anybody else tired?"

"No!" the others shouted.

There were leg lifts, more push-ups, and other things. Joey showed no mercy, making each task physically demanding. She could not afford to be soft on him -- her right to command was at stake.

Disobeying orders was a serious charge. Lives depended on everyone working together. They could not depend on each other if someone thought he could do whatever he wanted.

When the three days ended, Jesse collapsed on his cot in exhaustion. Joey got the next three days off to recuperate from Jesse's discipline. Everyone else, including Jesse, had to report for regular duties.

The next few weeks had the team taking one-and two-day trips away from camp. Those were called "lightning" expeditions. They would strike a target, then retreat.

One sunny afternoon, several weeks after Jesse's discipline, the Major assembled the team for another special assignment.

"It's about time we got some real action," Jesse complained.

As the team entered the tent, Joey announced, "All present and accounted for, sir!"

"I've got a special assignment for your team, Benson," Major Doyle announced. "I want you and your people to head deep into enemy territory. Your destination is their communications center. Come over to the map."

Everyone moved forward to study the map.

"Thirty miles from here," Major Doyle pointed, "is one of the enemy's main communications centers."

They watched with interest.

"Your assignment is to penetrate enemy lines and destroy this communications center. That will leave the enemy troops cut off from their central command, and our victory will be close at hand. The New Order will be victorious.

"Take enough explosive charges to flatten the entire center. You leave tomorrow at oh-four-hundred and will be behind enemy lines before sunrise."

"Yes, Sir!" everyone replied.

"Oh, and Burrows, I don't want to hear any more reports of disobeying orders. Is that clear?" He looked at Jesse.

"Yes, Sir!"

"Any final questions, Sergeant?"

"How do we get out of the area before the explosives go off?"

"That's up to you to figure out. Dismissed."

CHAPTER 6
THE HUNT

Reluctant to leave the safety of camp, Joey paused and glanced over her shoulder. It was her birthday, and she wondered there would be any future birthdays.

Will I ever see our home camp again? If I come back, I hope it's in one piece.

She had to accept the assignment. There were no alternatives. Anything else would be met with the severest of consequences. Pressing on to meet the team at the rendezvous point, she was lost in thought.

In these past months, I've seen more death and destruction than I care to remember. Her mind was controlled by the Militia's New Order. They told her what to think and believe, to compartmentalize any feelings that might occur. Ultimately the goal was not to have any feelings at all and certainly never to express them. To add to all this her mind was never free of the horrible scenes of reality.

No more killing! A small voice said in the back of her mind.

Killing is my duty! A louder voice replied.

Knowing her duty all too well, Joey had to listen to the louder voice and never waver. The past months made her feel like a killing machine sent to purge imperfections from the New Order. Faltering would mean destruction for her, and possibly, her grandparents.

Thoughts of them wandered into her mind. She wondered what they were doing.

Remember that we love you. Their last words echoed in her head.

"No!"

"Did you say something?" Randy walked closer, carrying a heavy case of explosives.

"Nothing!" Joey stammered.

Randy leaned over to whisper, "It's OK."

"What?"

"I sometimes reply to the voices in my head, too. Sometimes, I panic thinking someone else will hear the voices or me talking to them."

Joey stared at him. *Could there be someone else who feels like I do?* She wondered. She did not want to consider the possibility. The consequences would be too severe if she were wrong. She tried to ignore his words.

"We hear the voices," Randy said, "because we don't mesh with the programming. I don't always feel up to all this killing. I figure I have to kill in order to survive. We do what's expected of us until we find a way to beat it. When we do, we'll stop killing."

He made it sound so simple.

Joey stared at him in confusion and disbelief.

Was he for real or a spy?

"You and I aren't like the others," he whispered. "Our feelings are still part of us. They haven't been able to kill our emotional side. It's only hidden behind the New Order's programming. We have people who love us and care about us. That affects everything."

"What are you whispering about?" Jesse inquired.

"Nothing that pertains to you," Randy barked. "I got the explosives, sir! There's enough here to blow half the state to kingdom come."

"Good. You carry them," Jesse said. "That way, if anything goes wrong, you can be blown to bits. I'm not ready to die. I want to do some more killing first."

Joey eyed him suspiciously, "Each person carries his share," Joey ordered.

"What for? Let Matthews carry them."

"It's too heavy for him to lug the entire distance."

"Then let his brother help. Keep the losses in the same family."

"I said everyone carries some. I don't need to explain myself to you, just do it."

"Count me out. I refuse to be blown up." He stated as he stalked off.

"Get back here, Mister, and carry your share! That's an order!" She put her hands on her hips, daring him to disobey.

Jesse turned and slowly walked back. Defiance and hatred showed in his eyes, but he did not argue anymore. He accepted his share of the load with the others.

Joey decided it was the wrong time to worry about Jesse's threatening looks. She needed to stay focused on their mission. Joey led the team into the woods. The thought of heading so deeply into enemy territory made her heart beat faster and her palms sweat.

As they walked, each one carried their gun ready to fire. Hoping to get through enemy lines before dawn, Joey set a faster pace.

Then the sound of machine-gun fire sent them diving for cover.

"If that gun hits one of the explosive packs, we'll all be blown to bits!" Charlie panicked.

"Shut up!" Jesse barked.

"We have to destroy that gun before it tells the whole enemy army we're here," Joey said.

"Or worse," Randy added.

"You're the boss," Jesse mocked. "What will you order us to do?"

Joey glanced at Jesse, decided to ignore his disrespect, then said, "Thanks for volunteering, Burrows. You and Matthews, B. break off to the right. See if you can get close enough to destroy that gun."

"Are you sure? Maybe I should just map its location."

"You've got your orders. Follow them! Leave the explosives here for now."

Bobby and Jesse raced from tree to tree, moving steadily closer to the machine gun.

"Rogers and Jones, go left and see if you can keep them guessing which way we're coming from. Matthews, R. and I will give you cover."

Returning fire, they moved around, trying to keep the enemy confused. Bobby and Terry crawled along the trail, shooting. Suddenly, Jesse jumped up and ran toward the machine gun like a madman.

"Get down, you fool!" Joey shouted.

Jesse ignored her. He ran forward with a grenade in his hand, threw it and then hit the deck. Shrapnel flew everywhere as the grenade exploded, missing Jesse by inches.

When the smoke cleared, everyone got to his feet.

"I told you to destroy the gun, not yourself," Joey growled. "That was a demonstration of stupidity."

Jesse stood with one hand on his hip. The other held his rifle balanced on his shoulder. "Do I detect a note of concern in your speech?" He placed a hand over his head. "I'm touched."

"You had your orders."

"I obeyed them. What more do you want?" Jesse snapped.

"I want you to use your head and stay alive."

"Ah! You *do* care. It's touching really!" He struck his chest with his fist. "It gets me right here."

"Shut up. I don't want to be behind enemy lines with a team one man short, because he's an idiot."

Jesse glared at the word idiot. "Are you finished?"

"I'll tell you when I'm finished. If you live through this mission, I will place you on report, and that means further disciplinary action for you. Now I'm finished, and you're dismissed!"

Jesse turned away and mocked her, then he sat down defiantly under a nearby tree.

I shouldn't let him get away with that, but on the other hand, I don't want a confrontation with him behind enemy lines. Staying alive is more important.

Joey looked at the faces of her team members. They seemed eager to serve, but a little nervous perhaps. "Let's go." She looked at the map. "We should reach that communications center soon."

The team plodded on. They arrived at their target in midday without any further encounters with the enemy.

"We didn't meet much resistance getting here," Randy said.

"Maybe they're all on the front lines," Bobby added.

The team crawled forward to find an observation point.

"Maybe it's a trap," Charlie said with a voice that sounded like a whine.

Joey lay on an embankment and looked with her binoculars. "There it is.

Doesn't look too heavily guarded."

"How many?" Randy asked.

She looked again. "I count six. They must not think anyone would come this far behind enemy lines."

"Either that," Jesse said, "or they knew you were coming and ran off in fear. They must've realized they were no-match for your brilliance."

"Burrows, you will shut your mouth and keep your wise offs to yourself." Joey barked.

She turned to the team, "Here's what we'll do." Joey explained her plan, then added. "You'll only have a few minutes before the charges go off, so get as far from that place as you can. The Matthews twins will set the charges while the rest of us keep the guards busy. We'll regroup on this embankment after the explosion. Move out, and be careful."

They hustled into position. Using a series of soft whistles, they signaled their readiness.

Randy and Bobby set the charges in the designated areas. One by one, Joey and the others crept up on the guards and stabbed them in silence. Deep inside Joey wanted to run away, but she held in place by another force, that was now in control of her. Yet, she felt as though another forced their control over her. The knife slid into the guard's flesh. She felt his weight slump as the life drained out of him. The look on his face was beyond description as he dropped to his knees and then to the ground dead. As soon as all the guards were dead, the team dove for cover.

The explosion shook the ground like an earthquake. The force of the blast sent concrete, glass, and bodies flying through the air. A hand landed near Joey and made her stomach roll and her head spin. She took a deep breath and suppressed the urge to scream.

As the smoke cleared, Charlie screamed and leaped to her feet. A piece of a skull with the eye still intact landed near her.

"Shut up!" Jesse said. "Do you want the world to know where we are?"

Charlie kept howling and running in a circle. Joey never saw such a thing before.

"Jones, get control of yourself," Joey ordered. "You're going to get us all killed."

"No more!" Charlie threw down her rifle.

"No more what?" Joey asked trying to distract her.

"She's freaking out," Randy informed.

"Grab her and stick something in her mouth," Joey barked.

Before anyone could respond, Charlie bolted into the woods. She ran faster than Joey had seen her move.

"Get back here!" Joey shouted.

"Let's get out of here before this area's flooded with enemy troops," Jesse urged.

"We've got to go after her," Joey said.

"Why?" Jesse asked. "Let her go. We're better off without her. If she wants to freak out, fine let the enemy deal with her. Why do we have to pay for it?"

"Because I said so, that's why. Now let's go!"

The troops grabbed their gear and ran after Charlie. Joey led the way trying to catch up to Charlie. Her legs were moving so fast, she did not feel like she even touched the ground. Trees blurred past her. She weaved in and out of the trees searching for Charlie's trail.

"Here," Randy called.

They stopped to examine a broken branch.

"This is fresh," Randy announced. "I think she went this way."

"Or it could be an enemy patrol." Jesse added.

"Lead on." Joey said ignoring Jesse's comment. Randy took the lead, a little slower, followed by Joey and the others.

Joey felt like she was tracking an animal.

What made Charlie act like that? We've all had the same training. We've all been programmed the same.

Her heart pounded at the thought that any one of them might react the same way -- including herself.

"Spread out a little," she ordered.

The team expanded their search to cover a little broader area.

"Why can't we just let the enemy have her," Jesse said? "Anyone who acts that stupidly deserves to be captured. Let's go back to camp and celebrate our victory."

"Speaking of stupidity," Terry interjected, "have you thought about your actions with the machine gun? Maybe we should've left you, and not given you any cover."

"Maybe we should've left *you* behind," Jesse quarreled, "since you get so scared when a bomb explodes."

"Shut your mouth," Bobby snapped.

Jesse wheeled, ready for a fight. "Want to make me!"

"Kill the chatter," Joey ordered. "We don't need to be fighting among ourselves out here. Keep a sharp eye out for Charlie. I want her found, and then we're out of here."

Randy stopped to examine a footprint. "We're still with her–that's her boot."

"There's a clearing up ahead," Bobby announced.

As they entered the clearing, they spotted Charlie on the bank of a river. She was kneeling to wash her hands in the water. The group fanned out, moving cautiously to surround around her. They did not want to spook her into another episode. As Charlie turned to face them, her body was shaking. Tears were streaming down her face.

"Stop!" She pulled and aimed her pistol at them.

"You don't really want to shoot us, do you?" Joey asked trying to sound calm. "We're on your side, remember? We're the good guys!"

"Are you kidding?" Jesse asked. "We could cut her down before she got off a shot." He aimed his rifle at Charlie.

"Shut up!" Joey said. "Burrows, put down the gun! We don't need to make this incident any worse."

"Stay away from me," Charlie whimpered. "...I can't get them clean any more."

"Can't get what clean?" Joey inquired.

Charlie slowly raised the gun to her temple. "I don't want to do this any more."

"We can work this out." Joey inched closer.

"I can't do it anymore! I'm not a killer! I can't do it!"

"Put the gun down, and we'll go home together." Joey tried to sound reassuring.

"Right -- you'll send me to the Pleasure Farm when we get back. I don't need a bunch of sex-crazed men pawing me for the rest of my life."

"Killing yourself is not the answer," Terry added.

"Yes, it is." She took a deep breath. "I don't want to live in a world where soldiers are under the age of twelve and go to war and really kill people. Killing myself will stop the programming in my head."

Before Joey could move, Charlie pulled the trigger. Joey turned away quickly and bowed her head. *Maybe Charlie is right. There is no hope. We live in a world without it. . . .No, suicide can't be the answer.*

The team stood speechless around the body of their compatriot.

"Burrows, Matthews, B. dig a hole and bury her. The rest of you help." Joey ordered, breaking the silence.

"Why do I have to do it?" Jesse complained. "Why do we even bother? Leave her for the birds."

"We won't leave one of our own here to be salvaged for food! Get to work so we can get out of here!"

Joey walked to a tree and tried to pull herself together.

Rank had its privileges.

She watched the others dig and thought back to the only time Grandfather took her hunting. It was a few months before that dreadful day. The family was desperate for food, and the two of them relentlessly pursued a deer through the woods.

"I can't shoot it, Grandpa," she said. "It hasn't hurt anyone."

"It's OK, Joey." He took aim and pulled the trigger. "I have to kill it. We need the food. God gave us the animals for food."

Joey felt she had been forced to hunt again. This time, it was a human being, a child younger than herself. *Why?*

"Finished, Sir," Bobby announced breaking into her thoughts.

Joey knew her question would never be answered. She had a duty to do. "Let's go back to camp." And she would do it.

The walk back went without incident. No further enemy encounters. Once back in camp, they immediately reported to Major Doyle's office for debriefing.

The Major watched as they filed in.

"Where's Jones?" he asked.

Joey stepped forward. "Private Jones committed suicide behind enemy lines, Sir."

"Explain!"

Joey did so. Finally, the Major shrugged.

"A casualty of war," he said. "Perhaps it's better that way."

He did not even seem concerned. Joey knew he did not care about Charlie or any of them. His concern was for the duties they performed. Charlie was free. She had found a release.

While the Major debriefed them, a messenger ran in.

"Sir, central command reports the enemy has surrendered. The war's over!"

"Thank you, Private. Dismissed." He looked at the team. "You have done well. The New Order will honor your faithfulness and your responsiveness to your duty. Return to your bunker and pack! We will leave for our home base first thing in the morning."

They saluted and filed out. Joey walked to the bunker deep in thought. They were returning in one piece. She could not believe the war was really over, because it still raged inside her.

CHAPTER 7
STANDING DOWN

Returning to the compound, Joey climbed down off the truck and looked around. Everything appeared the same. Nothing had really changed, but she had changed. Her inner war became more intense. Not only was she no longer the laughing little girl with a ponytail, she was not even the gullible soldier she had been either.

She had seen the ugly, base side of humanity during the war. She tried to suppress all the unpleasant things she had seen and experienced since this whole thing began. She even tried telling herself it did not matter. As a result, her inner self seemed to wither away. It hurt too much to fight the Militia's brainwashing. Compliance meant survival, and survival was a necessity.

Caring about anyone or anything caused too much pain. The teachings of the New Order were too strong to fight against for very long. She decided it was best not to care.

Joey returned to her cubicle in the barracks. Everything was as she had left it. She went to the window and longed to be free like the birds. *Maybe Charlie is one of the lucky ones. She certainly is free from the abuse and humiliation the rest of us face.*

"Attention on deck!" someone shouted.

Joey ran to the opening of her cubicle and snapped to attention. Major Doyle walked into the room.

"You've done well, my Compatriots," he said. "We saw your loyalty to the New Order once again." He glanced at his prodigies. "Now that you're back, your families have requested an overnight visit. Because of your performance over the past few months, the New Order has decided to grant their request. We feel it will help stop the growing rumors that fuel the underground Resistance. You will be informed when this visit will occur." He turned and walked out.

Things returned quickly to their normal routine. During her morning academic classes, Joey learned she was on the promotion list. Normally, that would have been good news, but the higher one's rank, the more that person would be under the eye of the leaders and a target for other students. Although the other soldiers were loyal to their superiors, everyone coveted the higher positions. They watched officers for any infraction that might cause them to fall, then the informant would report them with hopes their reward would be to fill the vacant position.

Joey sighed and remembered the pressure she felt during her time as sergeant. It intensified when she was given command of an attack team. With the possibility of being promoted to lieutenant, the pressure could grow even more.

After classes, Joey went for a walk on the parade grounds, hoping the fresh air would clear her mind.

The autumn day was splashed with color. Serenity covered the whole area. Yellow sunlight stretched its warm light on red, yellow, and orange leaves. Stalks of corn stirred in the wind and whispered softly. The scene reminded her of a painting she once saw.

Suddenly, the serenity of the countryside was shattered by the blood curdling screams of eight young soldiers running toward her from all directions. Shocked at the scene, Joey looked around for a way of escape, saw none, and automatically went into a fighting stance.

The first member of the group leaped and tackled her, then all the others pounced. She was big and very strong for twelve, but she could not outfight eight trained super soldiers. They beat her until she gave up resisting.

Blood ran from her lip and down her chin. Large bruises formed on her face. Someone forced her hands behind her back, another tied her hands and yanked her hair until she knelt to the ground.

The soldiers turned their eyes toward the main building. Major Doyle was coming toward them. "Well done, Compatriots. You have honored the New Order."

He looked down at Joey. Her captors forced her head up until the sun blinded her. The Major's countenance became stern. In a harsh voice, he recited a long list of alleged crimes Joey had committed.

Joey tried to make sense of the situation. *What crimes? I haven't done any of those things you listed. This is a mistake.*

"Compatriots," Major Doyle finished, "you've heard the charges. What is your verdict?"

"Guilty!" they shouted in unison.

He addressed Joey. "You've been found guilty of crimes against our New Order. I sentence you to death. The sentence is to be carried out immediately."

Joey had no time to think. Fear and confusion swept over her, but she did not let anyone see. Remembering her resolve to never let the Major break her, she steeled herself to die. Teeth gritted, she glared at him.

At least I will be free.

Major Doyle pulled out his pistol and aimed it at her head. Terror filled her being as she stared into the barrel. She bit the inside of her lip to keep it from quivering and held her breath as his finger tightened on the trigger.

She remembered the movies they had seen of similar executions. When the movie got to this point, the gun fired, and the person died sending pieces of themselves all over the area. She gulped and wondered what it would be like to die. Maybe it would really be a release.

Major Doyle pulled the trigger. The gun clicked on an empty chamber.

She managed to maintain her composure, but her insides felt like gelatin. She did not flinch when the trigger clicked. She did not know if she was relieved or disappointed to still be alive.

The eight warriors untied her. It had been a test of some kind. They acted as if it were a game, laughing and joking as they sauntered away.

"I want to see you in my office in thirty minutes," Major Doyle ordered. "Clean yourself up and change your uniform before you come."

Everyone left. Joey crumpled to the ground in pain. As long as there was no one to see her, it was all right.

After several minutes, she pulled herself together enough to return to the barracks. She had been reprimanded for some small infraction earlier during her classes, but the reason seemed unclear. Then, she had been told of a possible promotion. Now this! Was this to see if she was worthy of the promotion? Had their programming done what they had planned?

Back in the cubicle, she had a few minutes to clean up before reporting to the Major. She assumed the meeting was to find out if she passed the test. Failure would make her future unbearable, while success would intensify their domination.

Uncertain of which she would prefer, Joey walked slowly to her appointment with destiny. Her body was complaining from the beating.

She was five minutes early -- always a good thing to do. The Major liked that. She knocked on his door.

"In!" he called.

She marched into the office and saluted.

"Sergeant Benson reporting as ordered, Sir!"

"At ease." He finished writing a report before looking up at her. "Benson, I've been watching you since the day you came here. Your loyalty to the New Order is commendable and, in many ways, unequaled."

Unequaled? That's a surprise!

"You served us well in the expansion war. In addition, your response to this afternoon's exercise was outstanding. None of our compatriots has been able to hold his composure as well as you did. To reward you, I have the honor of promoting you to lieutenant junior grade."

She knew this was an honor, but it was hard to feel happy about a promotion under these circumstances. Joey wished she could tell him what she thought of his so-called honor, but that would mean death or possibly worse. Instead, she recited the expected oath and waited to be dismissed.

Major Doyle pinned her new rank insignia on her uniform collar. "Congratulations, Lieutenant Benson!"

She stiffened at the sound of her new rank and saluted.

"Now that we've taken care of that matter, I've got a special mission for you."

"Yes, Sir!"

"You might say this is a pet project of mine."

"Sir?" She could not hide her surprise.

The Major walked to the window and looked out. "Do you know what the UDR means?"

"Yes, Sir. It means the Underground Democratic Reformation."

"Good." He seemed more relaxed. "What do you know of this movement?"

"Only what we've been taught in our classes, Sir."

"You're aware of the danger of this movement then?"

"Yes, Sir!"

"This group is seeking to overthrow our very way of life. It's a threat to our very existence." He glanced at Joey. "Are you familiar with the Eighteen-to-Twenty-Five Project?"

"Yes, Sir. That project selects women between the ages of eighteen and twenty-five and impregnates the ones who pass the screening process. The women are cared for until they give birth, then the offspring are taken and raised by our experts to be the next generation of super soldiers."

"Very good!"

Joey wondered what the underground Resistance and the project had to do with each other.

"Two months ago, while we were fighting the war, six of these women escaped. There was no one to go after them at the time. Now that the war's over, we must take care of this unfinished business."

"Yes, Sir!"

"We have information that the underground has them. If they're allowed to remain outside our care, part of the next generation of warriors will be lost."

Joey shifted nervously and listened.

"An informant has told us where the women are being hidden. Your mission is to lead your team in and reclaim our property. In addition to bringing back those women, you'll arrest anyone else you find there. We must teach them a lesson and squelch this movement."

"Where should we bring the prisoners?"

"Bring them here directly to me! The women will be returned to their dormitories until after they give birth. Any others will be punished severely."

"We're short one team member after the death of Private Jones, Sir."

"I assigned Corporal Steve Nelson to replace her."

"Understood, Sir!"

"One more thing, Lieutenant. I want you and your team to make those people regret they ever thought of associating with the underground movement. Do that before you bring them here, but under no circumstances will you harm the pregnant women. We don't wish to damage our unborn warriors. The women will be punished later."

"When should we go, Sir?"

"You'll attack the location as soon as you assemble your team. We don't want the underground to learn of our plans and move the women to another location. After you've completed your mission, you'll be free for the overnight visit with your relatives. Here's the address. Dismissed."

Joey saluted and left. It was her first assignment as a lieutenant, and she wondered if her team would be assigned this type of law enforcement duties on a regular basis.

Joey sat at a desk waiting, while her team assembled in one of the classrooms. She rocked back in her chair as she eyed each of them entering the room. There was now hardness in their eyes. Each had seen things that most adults only saw in their worst nightmares. She hoped she could keep them under control. They had tasted blood and many of them had liked it.

Steve Nelson was an unknown to Joey. She would need to wait to evaluate his strengths and weaknesses.

"We've been assigned to raid a known underground location," Joey announced. "Our informants have located some of the women who escaped from our next-generation dormitories. We're instructed to arrest anyone we find there. Under no circumstances can we harm the pregnant women -- our future depends on them. However, we've also been told to make everyone else we find sorry for being in league with such a dangerous movement. Any questions?"

"What happens to the women?" Terry asked with a concerned look.

"We bring them back to the Major. Beyond that, it's none of our concern."

The other team members gave Terry a threatening look, and she slouched lower in her chair. Her face turned red.

"It is our duty to defend the honor of the New Order. Their members of the Underground laugh at us and imply we are weak. We must go and take what is ours. We must teach them the lessons of fear."

"Yeah!" They cheered.

"The future of the New Order depends on the quality of the work we do today."

"Now, let's go out there and make the Underground Resistance regret they ever sided against us."

Joey rose and led the members of the patrol out of the room and off the base. Soon, they were standing in front of the house of the address she had been given. Steve used a special security badge to unlock the doors.

The patrol charged in and found the six pregnant women, as well as two other women and two men. The team members beat the four people. Their screams were deafening as they were hit and kicked repeatedly. Joey heard the sound of bones cracking, but she felt unmoved. During the fight, each member of the team showed their skill in combat. They kept beating the four underground members until they could not stand. Joey guarded the pregnant women so she would not have to hit anyone. Before long, each lay on the floor moaning and bleeding.

The pregnant women were sobbing, when suddenly, one of them screamed, clutched her abdomen, and sank to the floor. The compatriots stopped beating their victims and stood immobilized by the woman's shrieks. No one expected anything like that.

"Steve, call the base," Joey ordered. "Tell them we've got trouble."

Steve stared at the woman laying on the floor with her legs spread apart.

"Move!" Joey barked,

I don't think I should be seeing this.

Steve snapped out of his daze and ran to the phone. The woman screamed, arched her back, and lifted her pelvis. Joey's eyes doubled in size as panic gripped her.

"You can't have that baby now," she announced. "We don't know what to do."

"Tough luck, Kid," the woman gasped.

Being called a kid made Joey angry. "You can't have it now!"

"That baby's coming whether you want it or not." Sweat beaded on her forehead. She took a deep breath. "You'd better do something to preserve your precious superior race." The woman's cynical tone unnerved her a little.

"What should I do?"

"Lieutenant," Steve called, "Command says they can't get anyone here in time. They said, you need to handle it on your end - improvise if need be."

"How?" she snapped.

"They say to adapt. Besides, she'll do most of the work. You just stand by and assist as necessary."

Assist as necessary? How am I supposed to know what's necessary?

The woman bore down and pushed. After a long time, during which she screamed and took deep breaths, a black bulge began to show between her legs.

"Burrows, get some towels," Joey ordered.

On the next push, the baby's head came out. Instinctively, Joey reached for it and supported it with her hands. The left shoulder came next.

"Just yank the kid out!" Jesse said. "That'll shut her up. Then we can get out of here."

"Shut up, Burrows!" Joey lifted the baby slightly, and the right shoulder followed. A moment later, the baby was born.

"What a mess!" Jesse announced. "Yick!"

"I think you're supposed to stick your finger in its mouth and get out the crap," Randy said.

"Is it supposed to cry?" Bobby asked.

Joey nodded. She stuck her finger in its mouth and cleaned out the mucus, then the baby cried loudly. It was wet and squirmy, making it difficult to hold onto.

"Gross!" Terry said making a face.

"Just think," Jesse sneered, "you looked like that, too."

"So did you!" Terry retorted.

"Enough!" Joey wrapped the baby in the towels and placed it on the mother's stomach. She noticed the baby's foot seemed a little deformed and wondered what it would mean for its future.

66

After all my work to deliver the baby safely, the New Order would proba-bly kill it or make its life so unbearable it would wish for death.

There was no place for imperfection in this society.

Luckily, I don't have to make such decisions. All I need to do is obey or-ders.

"Tell command to send an ambulance for her," Joey said.

There was no point thinking about things. Nothing would change, so she had to make the best of the situation. Survival depended on conformity and obedience. Being different was dangerous.

"Tie up the prisoners and get them ready to march back to the com-pound," Joey ordered.

Within a few minutes, the ambulance arrived for the mother and baby. After they were gone, Joey led the team and prisoners back to the Major's office.

The beaten captives were barely able to walk, and the pregnant women supported them as they marched.

Isn't that a strange picture!

When they reached the Major's office, he greeted them with a rare smile.

"Attention!" Joey called as she shoved the prisoners to their knees. The team members fell in behind.

Major Doyle walked forward to examine the prisoner's injuries. He smiled as he fingered the bruises and broken bones, making the people wince or cry out in pain.

"Well done," Major Doyle announced. "It appears that you taught these rebels a good lesson. The Matthews twins will escort these five mothers-to-be to their dormitory at the northern edge of the compound."

The twins saluted and led the women away.

"I like seeing rebels bloodied," Major Doyle said. "You even broke a few bones. Very good!" He continued praising them.

Joey could not remember seeing the Major so pleased.

"Rogers, Nelson, and Burrows, escort this fly-spit to the detention cen-ter," the Major said.

The three soldiers saluted and yanked the ropes linking the prisoners. Groans of pain came as they shuffled out. Joey wondered what the Major planned to tell her.

She stood alone in the office, shifting her weight inconspicuously from one foot to the other.

"I just wanted to take the opportunity to tell you how pleased I am with your performance this evening," Major Doyle said. "You handled this mission in an exemplary fashion. If you continue like this, the New Order will have even greater rewards for you."

"For now, you'll be given more opportunities to serve. You can help us against the Underground. You're a perfect warrior." He paused to study her.

Joey felt the need to reply. "Thank you, Sir."

"Not at all!" Major Doyle glanced at the clock. "It will soon be time for the visits to the relatives to begin. We'll continue this discussion later. Please remind your people that visitation will commence at oh-nine-hundred tomorrow and end the following morning at oh-seven-hundred. Dismissed!"

Joey saluted and left. She returned to her cubicle and flopped down on the cot. Her body was exhausted, but her mind was on overdrive. The night passed slowly. The next morning after breakfast she changed uniforms and announced to everyone the return time. Relieved to know her confusion and questions were not detected by any of them. She prepared for the visit with her grandparents.

She looked around the barracks as many of the others prepared to leave. No one seemed happy about it. The longer they were in the training program, the more their relatives were strangers.

Joey assumed they were not being allowed to stay longer than one night in order to assure that each soldier would return for his daily injection. They still made her feel odd, and she wondered why they gave them. She wished she could stop taking them. Maybe that was why she could not remember her life before the New Order anymore.

As she left the barracks, the lower-ranking soldiers paused to salute her. She ignored them as she passed by. After taking a deep breath, she walked toward her grandparents' home. Her mind was confused. Thoughts came faster than she could process them.

Are we really standing down?. Is the war really over? I feel like it's only just begun.

CHAPTER 8
UNDISCOVERED TRUTHS

By the time she was halfway to her grandparents' home, Joey's mind drifted to thoughts about them.

Have they changed much? What'll they think of me? She grimaced. *Maybe I don't want to know! They've probably changed their mind about loving me. After all, look what I've become.*

The first one to greet her was her mother. "What happened to your face? It looks awful!"

Joey realized her face still had the cuts and bruises from the promotion test.

"Good to see you too!" She replied

"Put some cold water on those cuts." She went back to her sewing.

Joey walked into another room. There was not any point trying to discuss anything her mother. She felt like turning around and going back to camp, at least there she did not expect any civil words from them, but she wanted to see her grandparents, so she stayed.

It seemed as if a monster lurked in the shadows of her mind. Sightings of the beast made her shudder, and wondered if it really could be controlled or if it was only an illusion propagated by the Militia.

She went to the outside hand pump and washed her face. As she stood under a window, she overheard her grandparents talking. It was wrong to eavesdrop, but something held her in place.

"I don't care what you say, Jane, it's wrong!" her grandfather argued.

"Keep your voice down, old man, or we'll all be in a heap of trouble. Joey will be here soon. This discussion needs to be terminated before she arrives," Grandmother ordered. "Besides, you're not the only one. I'm as sick of this New Order as you are, but, if we say too much, we'll make trouble for Joey. I'm sure she's been through enough being sent to that awful war."

"That's another thing! Where do they get off sending a twelve-year old to fight in a war? And where do they get off deciding to change her name? How did we ever get messed up with such a group as this?"

"You're an old fool. You're the one who shot off your mouth about being dissatisfied with the government. Instead of looking for ways to support our government you helped get these dictators in control. As for sending our granddaughter to war, it's immoral, but you saw what happened to that man who stood up to oppose the Militia at the first meeting. Major Doyle let him die," her voice cracked as she swallowed a sob.

"So why can they play God? They have no right to do that. It's wrong, and we'll be judged for it."

"You sound like some of those folks in the Underground Resistance.... You're not involved in that are you?"

Grandfather did not reply.

"You better watch out, old man or you'll be the death of both of us."

"What are you two talking about?" Joey's mother asked as she entered the room.

Joey shifted her weight and listened, hoping no one heard her move.

"Have you seen Joey, yet?" She heard her mother's voice enter the room. The conversation turned to another topic, and Joey moved away.

Entering the house, her grandparents greeted her.

"It's good to see you again, Josephine," Grandmother said.

"My name is Joey!" She growled.

"I'm glad you agreed to visit us." Grandmother continued.

Joey did not respond. Her heart ached. Something inside tried to break through the ugliness of the past months, but it could not. The monster within controlled her thoughts and actions, so she acted in ways she did not want to act. Her grandparents seemed to feel awkward in her presence.

"So, what have you been up to?" Grandfather asked trying to make conversation.

Joey did not want to make small talk so she simply stared at them.

How can they still care about me? Don't they know what I've done? Af-

72

ter all, I've killed people. Ordered others into circumstances where they felt the only alternative was to kill themselves.

After several awkward moments passed, Grandmother asked, "What can I fix you to eat?"

"I doubt you have anything I'd like," Joey was shocked at her own words. *Who said that?*

Her grandparents looked at her in alarm.

"You seem different," Grandfather observed quietly

"I do? Maybe you're the ones who're different," she barked. Joey moved to a chair and fell into it.

"We're only concerned about you, because we love you."

"Who asked you to? I don't need you to love me. I don't need you or anyone else." Joey felt anger in her heart as the monster took tighter control. She stormed out of the room, leaving her grandparents standing bewildered in the kitchen. The war in her heart intensified.

"I told you to forget her," her mother said. "She's not your little granddaughter anymore, she's their robot."

Joey went to her old room.

Is it the beast inside that makes me act like this? Who's using my body? Why am I saying these things? I didn't want to be so rude to them. Maybe my mother is right. Maybe I am the Militia's robot. Maybe it would be best if they never see me again. At least I wouldn't run the risk of another visit like this, where I break their hearts?

Her mind was in continuous turmoil. She decided to go to bed but could not sleep. She only tossed and turned. Being in her old room and watching the shadows cross the room, brought old memories to her, but she could not focus on them.

What's happening to me? What does it all mean?

Thoughts haunted her as she lay in bed listening as the rain began to fall. It sounded like hot grease bubbling and crackling, ready to transform whatever it touched.

Will this monster consume me?

That thought tormented her as she finally fell into a troubled sleep.

The next morning, she woke feeling stiff and sore from the previous

73

day's beating and from the overly soft bed. She was still troubled by everything that happened. She decided to forget about the things she had overhead her grandparents say. The more she tried to push them out, the more they were in the center of her thoughts.

She dressed and ran downstairs, hoping to leave before she had to face her grandparents again. They appeared just as she was ready to slip out the door.

"Leaving so early?" Grandmother asked.

"I need to get back."

"I thought you didn't have to get back until seven o'clock," Grandfather said.

Joey did not reply.

"Can I fix you some breakfast?" Grandmother asked.

"No! I'm not hungry!" Seeing their hurt expressions, she added. "I...I don't want to make you short on food supplies."

"But you didn't have dinner, and now you don't want breakfast. You need to eat."

"I said I wasn't hungry. I need to go!" she shouted.

"I'm sorry you don't feel comfortable enough to visit with us." Grandmother sobbed. Joey felt uneasy and troubled that she had caused them further pain.

"I have new responsibilities and need to get back." Her tone softened slightly.

"You don't have to go back if you don't want to," her grandfather announced.

Grandmother looked at him in surprise.

Joey was puzzled. "Yes, I do."

"I can arrange it so you don't. You're troubled and confused. I can help you if you'll let me. I can take you some place where none of this will bother you again."

"You better shut up before you force me to report you." Joey snapped. Images from the raid flooded her mind. She remembered the terror on the faces of the people inside the house and the blood, the broken bones of those who were beaten. "There's no place to hide from the New Order," she announced.

"Yes, there is," Grandfather assured her as he moved a little closer to her.

"A lot you know." Joey growled.

"I can help you."

Joey stared, then she understood. "You're involved with them!"

"With whom?"

"Don't play games with me -- the Underground Resistance."

"What if I am?"

"It's illegal. People who are associated with them get hurt and often end up dead. It would be my duty to arrest you."

"You must do what your heart tells you." His eyes were filled with a special warmth. Joey saw that particular look in both of her grandparents' eyes but never in anyone else's.

Frustrated by her inability to make sense of things, she shouted, "Stay out of my way, or I'll have to arrest you!" She stormed out fighting to control the monster inside.

She hurried toward the academy thinking about the things that happened during the visit. She could not understand why such an intelligent man would become part of the Resistance. Even the Major said that Grandfather was a smart man.

She felt her grandparents watching her as she left, but the monster inside her would not let her look back. She felt ashamed of her actions. It was worse to know Grandfather was part of the Underground. She did not know what to do.

Duty demanded that she turn him in, but she could not force herself to do it. She decided not to do anything for the moment. Time would tell her what to do. She hoped that she would never have to face the possibility of arresting her grandparents. She forced the thoughts from her mind. She had other things to focus on.

CHAPTER 9
CIVILIZED SAVAGE

Major Doyle summoned Joey to his office early the next morning. Joey wondered now what. Thoughts flooded her mind as she arrived. "Lieutenant Benson reporting as ordered, sir!"

"At ease, Benson," he began. "I've got some questions for you. I'd like you to answer them to the best of your ability. What's your impression of Burrows?"

Joey could not imagine why he would asked for her opinion and wondered if her answers would get her into trouble. She shoved these thoughts aside. "Permission to speak candidly, Sir?"

The Major lifted an eyebrow, then nodded.

"Corporal Burrows is reckless and brutal, with a total disregard for authority." She didn't add, *for my authority*, but she wanted to -- that would sound too much like resentment.

"I agree."

"You do?" The words slipped out before she could stop them. Her eyes filled with fear and skepticism, and she braced herself for his wrath.

"Your observations are entirely accurate."

She could not believe it.

"However, I don't know many good officers who aren't on occasion a little daring. Sometimes, a little recklessness and brutality gets things done. That's part of being a good officer. It builds respect in those you command. It also shows the officer isn't squeamish. As for his disregard for authority, there's the possibility of turning that into something useful."

Joey tried not to show her bewilderment.

"The leaders and I feel he has the potential to make a good sergeant and eventually be given his own team to command. We'd like to promote him, but we have some concerns, too. We feel he needs to prove he's command material."

"How would he do that, Sir?"

"I can place him in temporary command of your team for a special assignment. Successful completion of that task would set the stage for other
command positions separate from you and your team."

"My team?

The Major nodded.

"What would I be doing while he's in command?"

"It would be awkward and wrong to have you under his command, so
you'll function as evaluator. You'd accompany the group and report on Burrows' performance and how the compatriots relate to his command. You
won't be subject to his orders, nor can you interfere. Even if he does something you believe is totally inappropriate, you can not intervene."

"Understood, Sir!"

"Be seated! I'll bring in the others."

Joey was surprised at his attempt at pleasantries. She sat and waited
nervously for the rest of the team to arrive. That was the first time she was in
the Major's office without receiving orders or punishment, and certainly the
first time she was offered a chair.

Major Doyle was gone only a few moments, he returned with the team.

Joey watched them file in. They looked at her and did a double-take as
they saw her sitting down. As she sat there, beaming with pride, she wondered if that was what life was about.

You do your job, don't cause trouble, and you get special treatment.

Her thoughts were interrupted by Major Doyle's voice.

"I'm assigning Private Jerry Martin as an additional member of this
team," he began. "Private Martin is nine and won a medal for bravery during
the war."

Joey thought Jerry looked small even for nine and wondered if he was out
of control like Jesse, or under control like the others.

"As you know," the Major continued, "the New Order has many enemies.
One of the biggest is the Underground Resistance. Those rebels undermine
our authority at every opportunity. They have no respect for our superiority...."

Joey listened to him and wondered why he felt it necessary to repeat these things so often. She decided either he forgot he told them to us, or he wanted to drill it into our brains.

"It's been reported that a woman with a chronic illness is being harbored by members of the Underground," Major Doyle announced. "They're treating her with illegal medicines and haven't reported her disease to the authorities. You know the regulations that mandate how individuals must report such illnesses."

He paused to glance at the team. "Lieutenant Benson has agreed to function as an observer for this mission. She will be our eyes and ears. Everything that takes place will be reported to us. During the mission, you'll take your orders from Corporal Burrows."

The corners of Jesse's mouth curled into a slight smile.

"Your orders are to enter the specified address, find the ill female, and execute her. We must show people that such things cannot be tolerated. There's no doubt how the New Order feels about such deception."

The team members glanced at each other. Joey wondered what they thought of an assignment to execute someone. She knew the New Order's reasons for killing the chronically ill, but it still did not feel right.

"One more thing," Major Doyle said. "Don't harm the other residents unless they interfere. We want them to know we can show mercy when it is appropriate. Those people are just misguided. We want them to know we're in control, and, by showing mercy to them, we demonstrate our ability to forgive. That will help us against the Underground's propaganda. Any questions?"

No one moved or spoke.

"That's all."

Jesse led the six members of the team with Joey following at a distance.

I wonder how well his orders will be followed. The team doesn't think too highly of him. . . . However, they are good soldiers and will do what's necessary to survive.

An early spring wind whistled through the budding trees outside. A late snowfall left a dusting of snow on the frozen ground. Jesse walked slowly but deliberately as he led his unit across a field. He wore a more pleasant expression for the moment, but that merely made Joey wonder what he was planning.

Jesse stopped to scan the countryside. He squinted at the afternoon sun, making him look older than twelve. After adjusting his cap, he continued leading the team.

When they arrived, Joey recognized it as the home of Jesse's family's. *I wonder if Jesse turned in his own family.*

"Halt!" Jesse said. "Matthews, R. and B. follow me in through the front. Nelson and Rogers, come in through the back. Martin, open the lock with that security badge, then stand guard out back. Be sure no one escapes -- Oh and Lieutenant, try to stay out of our way."

The team nodded.

Joey followed closely without responding to his remark. She did not interact with anyone. Randy glanced at her with concern. For some reason, she felt a special bond with him. There was no explanation of how or why.

"Be sure you're clear on our mission," Jesse said. "We're here to solve a community health problem. The chronically ill female is my aunt. She's forty-two and has tuberculosis. I learned this during my visit recently."

So that's how the major found out! Joey thought. *Jesse did turn in someone from his family. How could he?*

"In accordance with our health regulations, she must die. Health care for this illness is too costly. Don't harm anyone else unless they interfere. Is that understood?"

"Yes, Sir!" the team members said.

Jerry Martin opened the door with the security badge. Instantly, all the doors in the house unlocked, and the team burst in.

"Jesse, what's the meaning of this?" His mother looked up as seven young warriors entered her home.

"Shut up," he screamed. "Where's Margaret Burrows?"

"What do you want with her?" His mother demanded.

"You let me worry about that," Jesse quipped.

She eyed him. Jesse's brown eyes were wild. She turned and faced the rest of the team and saw their stern, youthful faces. The purpose of their visit suddenly dawned on her, and an expression of horror filled her face.

"How'd they find out? You told, didn't you?" She stared at Jesse. "How could you do this to your own family? What kind of a monster are you? First, your Uncle Jason's heart attack, now you're turning in your aunt for a death sentence?"

"She's already dead, now get out of my way!"

"No! Don't do this! You can't! Please, I beg you!" She looked at them intently.

Jesse pushed her toward Randy. "Hold her!"

Randy held her arms as she struggled. Jesse's mother was taller than Randy, but he was strong enough to subdue her.

Jesse searched the house as if looking for a mass murderer. His frenzy mounted as he ran from room to room. He intended to find his victim and prove his loyalty to the New Order. He was desperate to make a good showing.

"Stand by," he told the team. "I know this house better than any of you. I'll search. Make sure no one escapes."

As his search became more frantic, his mother fought harder to free herself. She shouted at Jesse to leave her home and forget it.

The scene reached beyond Joey's training and touched her heart. She had a mother, too, and would never put her through such a thing even if they did not get along.

Randy tightened his grip and held on, probably for the woman's protection. After he finished with a room, it appeared as if a tornado struck. The team members watched him with great surprise.

Suddenly, Jesse raced into the living room and slapped his mother repeatedly with the back of his hand until she fell to the floor. Joey watched and wished she could interfere.

Whatever happened to not harming the bystanders?

"Where is she?" Jesse demanded.

The look of frustrated anger in Jesse's eyes frightened Joey. She knew he could be brutal especially when he was out of control.

The sight of his mother crying on the floor made Joey's stomach ache. Jesse moved to hit her again, but Randy's powerful grip caught his hand in midair.

"Can't you see that her love for her sister will allow her to endure anything you can do?" Randy asked. "Don't take out your frustration on her."

"Need I remind you, Mr. Matthews, that I'm in charge of this mission?"

"Need I remind you, Sir, that our orders specifically stated no one was to be harmed unless they interfered?"

Jesse lowered his hand and went back to his search. Randy helped Jesse's mother up and steered her to a nearby chair.

"Bobby, get an ice pack for her eye," Randy called. Joey was surprised by his act of compassion. It was certainly out of character for these super-soldiers.

Bobby looked at his brother. When he saw Randy's determination not to let the assignment get out of hand, he obeyed. He returned a moment later and handed an ice pack to Randy.

"Put this on your eye," Randy said gently. "It'll keep down the swelling."

The moment was interrupted by a scream that could only mean that Jesse had found Margaret Burrows.

Jesse's mother jumped to her feet with renewed strength and ran toward the room. Randy made a half-hearted attempt to stop her, but she dodged him.

Before she could leave the room, Jesse emerged dragging his struggling aunt by the arm. Steve and Terry were right behind him, wrestling Jesse's cousin, who tried to escape through a window.

"Look who I found behind a panel in the closet," Jesse announced. "Hold her!" He shoved her into Bobby's arms.

Jesse's mother attacked him. He sidestepped and let her fall to the floor. "Don't force me to hurt you even worse. I have a job to do. Stand aside and let me do it. Then I'll be gone."

"If you think I'll stand by and watch you murder my sister, you're mistaken." She got to her feet.

Joey watched silently. Outwardly, she was calm, stoic, and uncommitted, but inside, she was in turmoil. Her stomach ached. She wondered how she would act if the situation were reversed. She did not know.

In her mind, Jesse was truly a civilized savage, a product of the New Order. His brutality was excessive, but Joey knew the Major would applaud it. She needed to be careful in her presentation and to not overemphasize his brutality. If she did, Major Doyle might feel she were getting soft, and her future would be in jeopardy.

Jesse's mother lunged again, managing to catch him off guard. She faked left, then moved right and she kneed him in the groin. He groaned, and his eyes bulged. He collapsed and grabbed himself. Joey chuckled to herself at the sight of this super-soldier being brought to his knees by an untrained woman. His mother had some good moves.

"Matthews, R., restrain her!" Jesse moaned.

Randy grabbed her before she could strike Jesse again. He pulled her back.

"Get your hands off me, you savage!" she shouted.

"Come back here and stand with us. You'll get yourself hurt! It'll be over soon!" He pulled her toward the doorway.

Jesse gingerly got to his feet, his eyes filled with rage. He slapped his mother repeatedly until her face was so swollen it became unrecognizable.

"Leave this alone, old woman, or you're next!" he screamed.

His mother shrieked and fought to free herself. Biting Randy's arm, she broke free and charged Jesse again.

This time, Jesse struck her with his fist hard enough to knock her backward. She landed on the floor in a heap. Jesse raised his boot, ready to kick her, but Randy stopped him.

"That's enough!" Randy placed himself between Jesse and his mother.

"Out of my way, you insubordinate pup! She is now interfering and deserves everything she gets."

"No. I said, that's enough. If you hit her again, you'll kill her. Your orders are to execute Margaret Burrows. Finish the assignment, and let's go. We've done more than we should have already."

"Do I need to remind you who's in command here?"

"I'm very well aware of that, Sir. You've reminded us at every opportunity. However, I'm filing a formal complaint against you for excessive and improper use of force. If you don't complete your duties now, I'll be forced to add that you exceeded your authority."

"You think you're smart, but your holier-than-thou actions will fry your butt." Jesse growled and brought his face within inches of Randy's.

Randy did not back down, staring into Jesse's face with fierce determination. He had enough of the senseless violence, and was ready to fight for a woman he did not even know.

Randy's actions stirred something deep inside Joey. She was not sure what it was, but she thought it had died long ago. A feeling rose that the monster within did not know how to handle.

"You'll get yours later." Jesse returned to the task at hand. He looked at his aunt and took out a formal document. "Enough interruptions! It's time we finished this."

Margaret cried and went limp in Bobby's arms.

"Shut up. This warrant states that Margaret Anne Burrows has been found ill with tuberculosis. It is in the best opinion of the New Order..."

"That's hogwash!" his cousin interrupted. "You're playing God, just like your kind did with your Uncle Jason."

"Don't start, old man," Jesse snapped. "It's in the best interest of the New Order to avoid costly medical care. Your illness is a burden to the government, you're sentenced to be eliminated at the hands of this enforcement unit."

"I hope you burn in hell for this," Margaret hissed.

"Were those your last words?" Jesse smiled and drew his pistol before walking toward her. Bobby stepped aside so the blast would not hit him if it passed through Margaret.

Jesse smiled as he aimed at her heart, and everyone held their breath. Then he pulled the trigger. The horror on Margaret's face burned deep into Joey's mind.

She slumped to the floor motionless.

"Rogers, check her pulse," Jesse ordered. "Let's make sure she's dead."

Terry moved forward as a bright red circle formed on the woman's yellow blouse. Suddenly, Terry ran into the bathroom and vomited.

"That's the last straw, Rogers," Jesse called after her. "You're through. I've had enough of your squeamishness. I can't believe you got this far in the program. Maybe you didn't have a tough enough leader." He shot a glance at Joey. "Nelson, you check it."

Steve moved to the body, knelt, and felt for a pulse. "She's dead."

"Then let's get the hell out of here." Jesse announced as he led the team out of the ravaged home. Joey lingered a moment to survey the damage. Jesse's mother crawled over to the motionless body of her sister. She gathered her in her arms and rocked back and forth as her body shook with sobs. John Burrows knelt beside the two women and wrapped his arms around them both.

The man began to sob as well.

The house was a disaster, the scene pulled at Joey's heart, as something tried to break through the walls she had built. When her throat started aching, she turned away.

"You're an animal!" Jesse's mother screamed to her son as everyone exited the horse.

Jesse paused in the doorway. "We'll send a truck for the body. We may be able to salvage something so the poor can have a few good meals."

"No!"

"You have no choice," he chuckled and then turned to leave.

The team was well on its way before Joey finally left the area. The sky was darker, and the wind colder. She wondered what to include in her report; she slowed her pace to ponder the words. She felt the need to defend Randy's actions. A wave of fear passed through her as she thought of Jesse being in command again.

"He's a good soldier," she muttered trying to convince herself, "and it would be a waste of talent to punish him too severely. Then there was Terry to consider. She has been given many opportunities to prove herself, and has always fallen short."

Joey knew she could not cover for Terry any longer without endangering herself. She wondered what to say.

When she arrived at Major Doyle's office, Joey slipped in and found everyone waiting.

"Benson, we've been waiting for you," Major Doyle announced. "I refused to take anyone's report until you arrived. The first report should be yours. Commence!" He sat on the edge of his desk waiting eagerly.

Joey shifted her weight and decided to stick to the facts. "We arrived at the house and entered immediately. Burrows became angry and beat the subject's sister without probable cause. He used unnecessary and excessive force, at which time, Matthews, R., issued a formal complaint regarding his actions.

"The subject was found, the warrant served, and the sentence carried out. Rogers was ordered to check the victim, at which time she lost control of herself and vomited. Nelson completed the order. Burrows ordered the team to depart, leaving the cousin and sister with the corpse. The house was left in a shambles."

"Matthews, R., your record has been outstanding so far," the Major concluded. "I applaud your strength in the stand you took, but caution you that such a thing could be viewed as insubordination. Nothing further will be said on this issue, except that I advise you to weigh your actions carefully."

Randy's worried expression dissolved into one of relief. "Thank you, Sir."

Jesse bit his lip in anger. Joey knew he was disappointed that Randy was not reprimanded for his actions.

"As for you, Rogers, I've had my fill of your weak attempts to fit in with our superior race. You have failed miserably each time. Nelson and Matthews, B., you will escort her to the detention center and remove her rank insignia. Lock her in a cell, we'll deal with her later."

Steve and Bobby obeyed.

"Please give me another chance!" Terry begged.

The Major's eyes were cold. "You'll have another chance to please us." He laughed. "But first, we'll wait until your shots wear off. That alone should give you some things to think about."

"No!" She screamed.

They dragged her down the hall, crying loudly. Joey reaffirmed her vow never to let the Major break her down, no matter what.

What does he mean until your shots wear off? What will happen then? I thought those shots were supposed to be vitamin supplements.

"As for you, Burrows, you're charged with excessive and brutal use of force. Do you have anything to say?"

"I did what was necessary to show them who was in control," Jesse answered. "If you don't start out tough, they'll walk all over you."

"A good officer doesn't need to prove himself constantly. I caution you against using such excessive force. While I applaud your ability to complete this assignment, I'm worried about the effect your brutality will have on your team and the community. The New Order wishes to keep the people under control, but when the means become excessive, we give the Underground more fuel to use against us. Do I make myself clear?"

"Yes, Sir!"

Joey felt a sense of delight as the Major railed at Jesse. He continued his lecture.

"Despite such a report," he concluded, "the New Order sees much potential in you. We therefore confer upon you the rank of sergeant."

Joey was caught by surprise. She thought surely Jesse would be found unfit to command.

"However, because of your past conduct, you'll be on probation for an indefinite period of time. Lieutenant Benson will resume command of the team and remain your commanding officer. Any further reports of excessive brutality will destroy your chances to command. We can't afford to aid the Underground that way. Understood?"

Yes, Sir." Jesse seemed a little sheepish.

Joey led them out of the office. Once outside, they scattered.

Joey got halfway to the barracks when she saw her name tag was missing. She retraced her steps. If the Major found it first, she would be in trouble. The same was true if she was caught without it.

She ran fast, searching the ground frantically. Her heart pounded as she came closer to the Major's office. Finally, she found it on the floor just outside his door. She bent over to pick it up, when she heard the Major's voice inside his office.

"We'd better cut back on Burrows' formula. He's a bit out of control. If he gets any worse, we won't be able to keep him under control." He chuckled.

"Which part of the formula should we decrease?" and unfamiliar voice asked.

"Cut back on the hormones a little but increase the mind control. Continue the present steroid levels. We want him to be the perfect killing machine. He'll be a good one to do our dirty work -- He seems to enjoy it so."

Joey gulped, then ran off. She did not stop running until she was back inside her cubicle. Memories of Margaret Burrow's face haunted her. Her mind shifted to questions about the injections they received; then it shifted to her grandparents. Desperate for tranquility, she went to the window.

She stared at the twinkling stars. They seemed to have the answers she sought, but she could not understand their language. Feelings she thought died during all of this programming were rekindled by the glimmering overhead lights. The events of the day stirred her in strange ways, until confusion overwhelmed her.

Joey swallowed hard at the thought that with the push of a needle, she could become just like Jesse.

CHAPTER 10
THE MISSION

Steroids. Hormones. Mind-control drugs. What does it all mean? Why are they giving us these things? Are the leaders of the New Order really playing God like Grandfather said? I don't understand.

Confusion filled Joey's mind as she prepared for bed. She longed for someone to share this turmoil with, but that was too dangerous. Besides, no one would understand what was happening to her. No one else is was experiencing the same things, so no one could grasp the magnitude of her situation. She doubted that even her Compatriots understood and she certainly would not attempt to share anything with them.

Joey felt she was being transformed into a different person. Maybe not even a person at all, maybe an unfeeling monster or a robot. The New Order wanted a super-soldier, a mechanical puppet to control the people. Such a soldier would kill without question, murdering babies and helpless old men and women.

Joey had killed people, too. She injured and maimed people, and perhaps enjoyed it a little. Did that make her a robot? She could not understand why there was such a need for so much violence. One thing was clear -- she had been chosen as one of these superior machines.

Sleep finally came, but rest did not. Instead, nightmares invaded her mind.

She was ordered to a house to uncover underground activity. Joey led her team in, breaking up the meeting and severely beating anyone she found. Laughing when they cried out in pain, she would hit them again.

"I'll teach you to be part of the Underground!" She prepared to hit an old man, when the face before her changed into her grandfather's.

"No!" Her voice woke her.

Randy crawled over to her. "Are you OK?" His voice blended with the whispers of the night.

"I'm fine." She was sweating and felt disoriented, but did not want anyone to know.

"Are you sure? If I can help, let me know," he whispered.

"Why do you say things like that?" She was shocked at his words.

"Let's just say I'm wise to what's going on in this place. I've got the leaders pegged, and I know what they're doing to us. The vitamin supplements, the whispers of the night, I know their true meaning. The first chance I get, I'm out of here."

"Why are you telling me? I could turn you in!"

"You could, but you won't," Randy sounded confident.

"What makes you so sure?"

"For the same reason you didn't turn Rogers in for wetting her pants or Burrows for punching you. You've got a heart, and you still care about people. You can't get away from it."

His words stirred up things in her she did not understand.

"You and I are kindred spirits," he continued. "Even with the drugs and brainwashing, you're not completely under their control. Me, either. Maybe something in our physiology that counteracts part of their drugs." He looked around to see if anyone else was stirring. "I'd better get back to my space before someone realizes I'm out of bed and gets suspicious." He crawled off, leaving Joey with more things to ponder.

Why would he tell me those things? Is he really a kindred spirit, or is he a spy trying to trip me up?

Chirping birds woke Joey the next morning. Their songs tried to send a tranquil message to her troubled soul, but it refused to be comforted. Too many things crowded her mind; her head felt ready to explode.

Before she finished dressing, she got a message ordering her to report to the Major's office before breakfast. Panic set in, and her legs shook.

What does he want with me this early in the morning? What have I done? I can't think of anything. Maybe someone reported last night's conversation with Randy. Or maybe he found out that I was outside his office and over-heard the conversation.

She went to the Major's office and was immediately ushered in.

"Lieutenant Benson, reporting, Sir!"

"Are you familiar with the Underground movement in this quadrant?" He sat at his desk staring at a piece of paper and tapping a pencil. He seemed unusually irritated.

He asked me the same thing when he sent me after the pregnant women.

She did not voice her confusion. She simply gave him the information again. "Yes, Sir. A group of rebels seeks to destroy the New Order by encouraging dissension in the ranks and by harboring fugitives."

"You realize they're dangerous? We feel we can't tolerate them any longer. We're ready to seek out and destroy anyone involved with them. We must end this poison in our society." He seemed almost crazed. "We've been patient far too long. The New Order is strong now, so we no longer need to worry about their rumors and propaganda. You and your team have been selected for the task." He studied Joey's expression.

"I summoned you early, because I want you and your team mentally and physically prepared for this special task. We have information that a secret meeting will occur at 1800 hours this evening. Assemble your team and go to this address. You'll use this security card to gain access to the home and surprise those inside. Arrest everyone you find."

"Yes, Sir!"

The Major handed Joey a piece of paper with the address and a security card. "One more thing, Lieutenant. This will be a difficult assignment. While you are there, make every one of those people regret they ever decided to attend that meeting. Don't bring them to me until you teach each of them a severe lesson."

"I'll be waiting for you and your prisoners. After breakfast and your daily shots, report to the training rooms. The six of you will be excused from regular academic classes today. Instead, you'll work out in the gym, get some extra rest, and watch special training films. Is that clear?"

"Yes, Sir!"

"Dismissed."

Joey turned and walked out. She glanced at the address, but it was not any place she knew.

Why would this be a difficult assignment? Why would it be any worse than the previous ones?

After stuffing the piece of paper into her pocket, she went to breakfast.

"Burrows, Matthews, B., Matthews, R., Nelson and Martin," a voice over the public address system called, "meet with your commanding officer in the weight room after you finish in the infirmary."

Joey wondered what the Underground was doing to subvert the New Order. She knew they harbored pregnant women who escaped from the dorms and sent out worthless propaganda on the evils of the New Order, but she wondered if there was something more.

Grandfather wouldn't be involved with anything illegal. Would he? No, of course not. Why are the leaders so against that movement? Do they fear it?

The day passed slowly. The team members were excused from their classes so they could work out in the weight room. After exercising, they rested and then watched training films designed to stir their fighting senses until it caused extreme physical tension. The release of that tension would come when they broke up the Underground meeting.

Finally, it was time to gather and make their final preparations.

Why does the Underground have to exist? Things would be easier if it didn't. Is there something about the old way that people want back? Didn't they want the New Order originally? Why did they change their minds? The New Order was created because of dissatisfaction with the government. Why would anyone want to go back under a faulty government? It doesn't make sense.

An hour before they needed to leave, the team met in an empty classroom. Joey sat in the teacher's chair and rocked it back on two legs. She watched the team file in and take their seats. They were some of the Militia's finest. Each was ready to die for it, and their loyalty was unquestioned. They were strong and ready to perform.

Is this what other ten-to-twelve year olds do?

The team members eyed her expectantly, awaiting a final pep talk. Such talks were designed to work them into a final frenzy. They would then be ready to kill on command.

Still, even with the working out and the movies, something nagged at Joey's mind about the mission. She was not fully under the monster's control, which left her feeling uneasy. Her heart was not in it, and she could not think of anything to say. Instead, she emphasized their orders.

"All right," she finished, "let's move out."

"You call that a pep talk?" Jesse challenged. "I got more excited when I wet my pants as a kid."

"Shut up!" Joey snapped.

Jesse's anger overcame him. He was so stirred up. He was ready to take on anyone. Joey was in the right place. He barked, "Let's have it out right now."

"Save your energy for the mission." Joey kept walking.

Jesse lunged. Before Jesse could reach Joey, Randy and Bobby stepped in and managed to subdue him.

Joey turned, angry and frustrated. "I ordered you to save it, but you had to push."

Jesse fought to break free.

Joey slapped him hard. It felt good. "You want a pep talk? I'll give you one. Your energies are to be focused on the enemies of the New Order. If that's a problem for you, we can work out something else, but it won't be a very pleasant alternative, I promise. Do I make myself clear, Burrows?" She slapped him again.

Jesse was stunned by Joey's aggressiveness. He nodded.

"Let's move out and get this over with." Joey was amazed by her actions. *Why'd I react like that? Is the monster finally taking full control?*

The twins released Jesse and he quickly adjusted his uniform and went to the rear of the group. Joey eyed him, knowing he would explode soon enough. If the doctors had changed the dosage of his injections, she did not notice a difference.

Joey led the team to the address. They crept up to the house, then Joey ran her security card through the lock.

Bursting in through the front door, Joey was followed by Jerry and Bobby. Jesse came in through the back door with Steve and Randy at his heels. They caught twelve people at the meeting completely unaware. All seemed frightened by the fierceness of the security team, and huddled together.

Jesse looked at Joey anxiously, awaiting the order to beat the rebels senseless. Feeling strangely nervous, Joey nodded for them to begin.

The team members beat the people mercilessly. They screamed. Jesse laughed as he hit a woman. Randy and Bobby took turns slapping a few of the people around, but Joey saw Randy did the minimum, just enough to make himself look good.

Looking at the rebel's faces, Joey saw fear in their eyes. She hated anyone who betrayed their feelings. Their terror unleashed the monster within her. She was about to release her frustrations by joining the fight when she saw Steve drag a familiar figure out of the bathroom.

She froze. Steve entered pulling her grandfather by his hair. Steve shoved the old man across the room. He stumbled. He fought to regain his balance, but he landed at Joey's feet. She stared down at him. The action stopped as everyone turned to see her reaction.

Joey felt sick as she gazed down at her grandfather.

What can I do? A war raged inside of her.

As she looked into his worn face and warm eyes. The teachings of the New Order were suddenly ambushed by some feelings for her grandfather.

In order to protect herself and keep face, she had to do something -- at least kick him. That would start the action again, and everyone would be satisfied. She picked up her foot and was ready to kick him, but her heart rebelled. Despite the drugs, brainwashing, and ugliness that tried to control her, something reached beyond the inner walls of her heart and mind. She could not hurt him.

"Hit him!" Jesse yelled.

"Hit him!" Steve added.

"Do something!" Jerry said.

"Hit him, or I'll see that you're finished!" Jesse threatened.

Even hesitating would cost her. Her thoughts returned to her grandfather.

The minimum penalty he would get was time in a prison camp. Things had a way of happening to people inside those camps, especially to political prisoners. She would probably never see him alive again if he were sent there. Tormented by that thought, she could not force herself to hurt him.

"Hit him!" Jesse ran over and kicked the old man.

Joey lunged at him and pushed him away. "He's mine! You stay out of this!"

Henry Benson rolled on the ground clutching his abdomen gasping for breath.

Jesse retreated, but he was still suspicious.

"Enough!" Joey ordered.

The team stopped beating the people.

"Chain them up. I'll take care of this one. Let's move out." Joey knew those were probably her last orders, but the team was obligated to obey her. Refusing to beat her grandfather would bring severe consequences. Even worse, she stopped another team member from carrying out his duties. She was finished.

They'll bust me to private at the very least. They will probably give Jesse command of my team and over me. The Major could send me to the Pleasure Farm, but first he would do everything in his power to break me, and I cannot let that happen.

The constant killing and beating seemed senseless. Until now, she had not had any ideas about how to stop it.

While the team members busied themselves tying up the captives, Joey grabbed her grandfather by the arm, pulled him to his feet and dragged him out the front door.

"Come on!" she hissed.

Henry hurried to keep up. He was still trying to catch his breath from Jesse's kick. Luckily, he was in good health.

They made it halfway across the nearest corn field before anyone noticed they were gone. Jesse shouted, "After them!"

Joey looked back and saw Randy casually standing in the door, blocking Jesse. That gave Joey enough time to get her grandfather into the nearby woods.

"Why'd you do this?" Grandfather demanded.

Joey stared. "Let's just say I followed my heart."

Grandfather reached to hug her, but she recoiled in fear. He settled for patting her on the shoulder. "That's my little girl."

Joey looked at him in confusion. "We've got to get out of here."

"Not without Jane."

Joey nodded. She knew her grandmother was in danger. If they captured her, they would torture her and possibly send her to the Pleasure Farm to get even with Joey and her grandfather. They had to reach her before anyone knew what had happened. The team would probably report the incident to Major Doyle before getting further instructions and a new leader. They might have enough time to rescue Grandmother.

"We'll have to hurry." Joey led the way toward the house. They darted from tree to tree, hoping no one saw them.

"Joey, go on and save yourself," Grandfather said. "You're faster than two old people. I'll get your grandmother."

"We're in this together. I won't leave without you."

"You need to think what they'll do to you if they catch you. You're a bigger prize than either of us."

"I'm thinking about you. If they capture you, they will use you to get to me. They have ways of getting information and most of them are very unpleasant. The past year I've been killing people simply for being sick or because the New Order wanted more territory. I've seen violence beyond your worst nightmares. Now I've made a decision and we all have to live with it. So, don't thank me for having a selfish attitude."

Henry smiled and stopped arguing.

They arrived at the Benson home and slipped in through the back door.

"Jane?" Henry called softly.

They moved from room to room, looking for Grandmother. Joey was worried they might be too late. Suddenly, Joey saw Randy sitting in the living room with Grandmother and jumped back in shock.

"Don't try to stop us, Matthews, or I'll kill you." Joey took a fighting stance.

"Relax, Chief. I'm on your side," Randy announced.

"Why should I believe you? You could be trying to make points with the Major by capturing me single-handedly for all I know."

"I told you I'd leave as soon as I found a way out. You're my ticket. I couldn't do it alone, and neither can you. Now, neither of us needs to."

"He's telling the truth," Grandmother added. "He came here and told me the same things."

Joey relaxed a little. "We'll need a plan."

"We should stick to the forest until we reach the lake," Randy suggested. "Once there, we'll grab a boat and head north and reach freedom."

"It sounds too easy," Jane said.

"It's workable," Henry added.

"It's all we've got," Joey admitted. "There'll be a team hunting for all of us, and the border patrols will be on alert."

"What about your mother?" Randy asked.

"She'll be OK," Joey replied. "She never associated much with me, and she can claim she didn't know about Grandfather's activities."

"OK. Let's get going."

They left through the back door and darted into the woods. They were leaving everything behind, while risking death for a chance to be free.

CHAPTER 11
IS THERE ANY ESCAPE?

The small fire danced and popped under the dim moonlight. Henry, Jane, Joey and Randy sat huddled nervously around the fire listening to the night noises. Randy occasionally stirred a pot of mushroom soup with his knife.

"It's a good thing we found those wild mushrooms and onions in the forest," he announced. "It's not like the special diet we normally eat at the academy."

"At least it'll fill your stomachs," Grandmother added. "Of course, it doesn't compare to my homemade soup."

"Nothing matches your cooking, dear." Grandfather beamed.

The sound of twigs snapping sent everyone into the bushes for cover. They hid behind trees and rocks and held their breath. After a few moments, they dismissed the sound as a passing animal and slowly returned to the light and warmth of the fire. Silence weighed heavily on them as they sipped the tiny bit of coffee they brought with them.

"Aren't we a fine lot?" Grandfather chuckled.

"Will we make it?" Grandmother asked worriedly.

"Joey, you know these people better than any of us. Do we have a chance?" Grandfather inquired.

"I don't know," she replied. "Major Doyle seemed more enraged than usual about the Underground when he sent us on that mission. I'm afraid this incident will be like pouring gasoline on a fire. Jesse will probably be put in charge of the team, and the Major will tell him not to give up. He's relentless enough on his own. With the Major behind him, our chances are slim."

"They might be even become slimmer," Randy announced. "Your chances might be better without us around."

"How so?" Grandfather asked.

"I'm guessing sometime around tomorrow afternoon, Joey and I might become more than you're accustomed to dealing with."

"I don't understand," Grandfather said.

"Major Doyle and his cronies have been giving us daily injections of various drugs. I'm guessing that without them, we'll go through some severe withdrawals."

"Are you certain?" Grandfather was outraged.

"I was assigned to take various youth who fell out of favor to the brig where I heard many going through withdrawals, some really bad."

"I heard Major Doyle say the same thing to some of the other leaders," Joey added. "He said that the right mixture of some these drugs controlled our behavior."

"What! That explains the changes in your behavior. That also explains how he could brainwash you children so quickly." Grandfather was furious.

They chatted long into the night. The embers of the fire died as dawn came. None of the fugitives could sleep that night.

"We'd better get moving," Joey announced. "We need to get far from here, and make good time before the inevitable happens."

"We need to cover our tracks," Randy said, "or we'll be captured fast."

"Agreed. Grandfather, kill the fire and scatter the ashes. Grandmother, use a branch to sweep our tracks from that side of the camp. Randy and I will do the same over here," Joey ordered.

All was taken care of, so they started hiking through the woods. They moved in a zigzag path to make it harder to track them.

In the afternoon, the warm rays of sunlight brought comfort to them.

"Randy, you don't look too good," Joey moaned.

"You should take a look at yourself."

"I feel awful," she agreed.

"We need to find a place to hide for the next few days." Randy said as he looked up at the sun.

"He's right," Joey told her grandparents. "This is your last chance to strike out on your own and get ahead of the search party."

Grandfather shook his head.

"Don't say I didn't warn you. You two will have your hands full. I apologize in advance for anything we might say or do."

"Yeah!" Randy agreed.

Grandmother and Grandfather were puzzled but wanted to help.

"This is your last chance to leave us behind," Randy said. "Your odds of freedom would increase."

"No." Grandmother insisted. "Absolutely not! You've been in the hands of those tyrants long enough. Your family will care for you now. We stand or fall together."

"That's right," Grandfather said.

Joey chuckled at their resolve. They would never leave them behind no matter what. Her thoughts started fading in and out, and she knew the injections were wearing off. Withdrawal would strike soon. The thought of being out of control frightened her almost as much as the fear of the drugs being in control.

Their only hope was to stay ahead of their pursuers. Heading for the lake was a logical thing to do, but she feared they would never make it.

They continued their zigzag course for a few more hours, but Joey and Randy soon were unable to keep up the pace. Perspiration fell heavily from their faces. Their legs felt like rubber as they staggered along. Their faces were flushed with fever. Physically they were going downhill fast.

"We need a place to rest," Joey said. "We can't go on, I feel awful."

Unable to find shelter, they kept on. Grandmother and Grandfather supported each of the super-soldiers as they grew weaker by the hour. Finally, Grandfather took charge.

"We'll stop here," he announced. "I'll build a small shelter from some branches. It won't be much, but it'll give you some protection from the elements. We'll be able to take care of you better there."

"We need to be farther away," Joey pleaded. "Jesse's like a dog that won't give up the scent until he's got us."

"I'm too out of it to argue." Randy collapsed to the ground. "I can't go on."

Grandfather quickly made the lean-to. Joey sat down and held her head. Soon chills took hold of them. Feelings of frustration, loneliness and anger overwhelmed Joey and Randy. A deep undefined craving controlled their bodies.

"She's burning up with fever." Grandmother touched Joey's forehead. She wrapped her coat around her granddaughter.

"Randy is, too." Grandfather took a handkerchief and poured some water from the canteen, then he dabbed Randy's forehead.

"Oh!" Joey grabbed her stomach and vomited. Her nerves twanged with excruciating pain from her toes to her hair.

"What can we do?" Grandmother asked. "Is there no escape from this New Order? It seems even when the children aren't with these people, they're still held hostage."

"All we can do is keep them cool," Grandfather. "Whatever those drugs were, they seem to have some nasty side effects."

"True!" Grandmother agreed.

Both young people took turns wretching, shaking and moaning.

"I'm concerned their calls will attract unwelcomed visitors." Grandmother added.

"Maybe it'll help quiet them if I read to them from this." He held up the Bible. "It can't hurt, and it'll help to pass the time." She looked at him with a puzzled look. "I hid this from the book burners."

Grandmother smiled.

As the hours passed, Joey and Randy vomited several more times. Their skin became flushed and pink.

"Major Doyle please take me back. I give up just give me something for this." Joey cried.

"And God shall wipe away all tears from their eyes; and there shall be no more death, neither sorrow, nor crying, neither shall there be any more pain, for the former things are passed away..." Grandfather read.

"No, Charlie!" Joey screamed. "Don't shoot!"

Grandmother held Joey as she twitched and rolled, and gripped her stomach as the cramps hit repeatedly.

"Jesse, get down!" Joey felt pain everywhere in her body.

Grandfather kept reading from Revelation. "He that overcometh shall inherit all things: and I will be his God, and he shall be My son..."

After a while, he said, "I don't know if they understand what I'm saying."

"It gives them comfort just to hear your voice," Grandmother said.

The children's temperatures continued to rise. Finally, they fell into a restless and troubled sleep.

"They've been through hell this past year," Grandmother said.

"Perhaps. It seems this journey will continue a few more days."

Night shadows came. Grandmother and Grandfather took turns sleeping, but every sound of the night woke them.

"No more!" Joey pleaded. "Please help me!"

"Kill the fly-spit!" Randy screamed.

"Easy, Son." Grandfather pushed Randy down.

The two continued raging with fever throughout the night.

As dawn came, Grandfather looked around. "Danger's lurking nearby. I feel it."

"Perhaps they'll be better today."

Joey cried out in pain. She and Randy started vomiting again. Grandmother had trouble controlling Joey's violent outbursts. Grandfather did not do much better with Randy.

Three long days passed. Finally, on the fourth day, Joey sat up weakly. Her head pounding.

"You look like you feel better," Grandmother announced.

"Oh, my head." Joey held it in her hands.

Randy struggled to rise. "We need to move on. They had plenty of time to catch up to us by now. I feel them nearby."

"You aren't ready to travel," Grandfather shook his head.

"There's no choice," Joey replied. "We can't let them catch us." She struggled to her feet and nearly fell over.

Grandmother rushed over to catch her. Grandfather grabbed Randy. They pressed forward, leaving everything. The adults needed to almost carry the children. No one took time to erase their tracks or destroy the lean-to. If Jesse and his group came this way, they would have no difficulty following their trail.

Joey fought to keep moving. Every step was agony. She felt sorry for her grandmother, but her mind could not focus on anything for too long. They had to figure out a plan of escape. When she glanced at Randy, he did not seem to be in any better condition.

In the distance, she thought she heard voices, but her mind wasn't clear enough to discern the direction.

"I need water," Joey begged.

"Henry, we must stop," Grandmother announced. "Joey needs water, and everyone could use a rest."

"OK, but hurry. I heard voices." Grandfather leaned Randy against a tree and passed around the canteen.

"Cover our tracks," Joey said groggily. "Change direction!"

Grandfather broke off a branch and swept the ground.

"Keep moving!" Randy groaned. The adults continued dragging the super-soldiers, who were nearly unconscious.

As the day wore on, Joey and Randy were able to eat some berries and feel some better. They were able to walk almost unassisted, and the group made a little better time. In the distance came the sound of hunters. From the sounds, Joey thought they were right behind them.

"We have to move faster," Joey ordered.

They ran, but they could not keep that pace for long.

"They're coming," Randy announced.

"We can't outrun them," Joey admitted.

"We'll be trapped soon."

"There must be something we can do." Grandfather said. "We've come too far to be stopped now."

"I'm sorry for causing you all this trouble," Joey said. "If it weren't for us, you two would've been days away."

"It's not your fault. If we hadn't been there, you two would've died. We couldn't enjoy our freedom knowing we left you at the time you needed us the most," Grandmother comforted.

"If it wasn't for us, you'd be safely over the border by now." Randy replied.

"Standing around arguing won't get us any farther away," Grandfather announced.

"We have to outwit them," Joey said. "Perhaps we can come up with a way to save some of us."

"No," Grandfather said. "We're in this all together."

"We have to do something to save some of us, or this has all been for nothing. Besides, those who make it through can spread our story around and might be able to save others."

"Let's split into two groups and take two different directions," Randy said. "It's not like Jesse to divide his team. That way, one group will have a chance of freedom."

"I don't like the idea of separating," Grandfather said.

"There isn't much choice or time. In order to have any hope of freedom, we have to split up," Joey announced.

"How should we do it?" Grandmother agreed. "I still don't like the idea, but I guess we have to try it."

"Since both of us are trained in these things," Joey remarked, "it would be best if we paired off with an adult."

"I'll go with Joey," Grandfather decided.

"Is that OK with everyone?" Joey asked.

"As much as I don't want to leave either of you," Grandmother said, "it's for the best. Maybe, by some quirk of fate, we'll be reunited in freedom."

"At the very least, we'll meet in heaven," Grandfather added.

Grandmother kissed her husband good-bye, knowing that there was every possible chance that she would never see him again. When she tried to kiss Joey, she cringed. Joey did allow her to put her arms around Joey's shoulders. Grandmother turned away quickly to hide her tears.

"We'd better get going, Randy," she said sadly.

"Good luck," Randy wished.

"Take good care of her," Joey said.

"I will."

They separated. Joey and Grandfather hurried through the woods, trying to cover their tracks.

"I'll miss that woman," Grandfather announced sadly.

"Maybe you should've thought about that before you got involved with the Underground." Joey rebuked.

"I understand your bitterness...."

"You don't understand anything about me!" Anger filled her. "There wouldn't have been any good-byes if you hadn't joined the Underground."

"Perhaps you're right! Whatever happens, I want you to know that I will never stop loving you."

"Why?"

Their argument was interrupted by a shrill whistle from behind.

"Let's move," Joey said.

"They've seen us," Grandfather added.

They ran faster. The thunder of their feet hitting the ground echoed in Joey's ears. That noise was eventually joined by the shout of others coming up from behind. Grandfather's age and Joey's weakened condition prevented them from outrunning anyone.

Suddenly, the tracking team was upon them. Jesse wrestled Joey to the ground. She was easily subdued, but he kept hitting her. He was enjoying his superiority.

Sitting astride her chest, Jesse slapped her face several times. "Where are the others?" He demanded.

Her silence enraged him. Jerry and Steve held Grandfather, who tried to rescue Joey.

"I'd finish you off right now," Jesse laughed, "but I promised Major Doyle I'd bring back enough pieces for him to have some fun, too. Get up!"

Joey lay on the ground and stared. Jesse looked fiercer than she remembered. Between her weakened condition and a defiant attitude, she refused to move.

"I said get up!" Jesse grabbed her shirt and yanked her to her feet.

The team members watched in silence. Their faces betrayed their mixed emotions about Jesse's brutality.

"Let's move out," Jesse ordered. "At least we've got these two. They're the most important. We've got the former hotshot of the Youth Army and a primary Underground leader. Should get a big reward for this." He smirked.

They escorted Joey and Grandfather back down the path. Joey was relieved to know Grandmother and Randy were safe for the time being. Even if another search party went after them, they would have enough of a head start to reach the border.

Her heart ached at the thought of never seeing them again, but there was some comfort in knowing they were free and could start a new life. They would never have to deal with the New Order again and never face the Militia's hostility.

CHAPTER 12
USE BULLETS

A loud commotion in the hall disrupted the New Order's panel of advisors. These advisors were established as a layman's government. They were controlled by the presiding military leader. In this sector, it was Major Doyle.

Their headquarters was located within the training compound. Major Doyle summoned these leaders to decide the fate of Joey Benson. They would probably try to make an example of her because she was the first to try to defect. She would be given a trial, but it would be all for show.

Joey stood before the panel as the commotion in the hallway came closer.

"Let me go!" Joey heard the familiar voice of her grandfather shout.

He burst into the room dragging two young people behind him. They were trying in vain to subdue him. Grandfather may have been in his sixties, but his work in the factories had given him enormous fortitude. The two guards with all of their drug induced strength were unable to control him.

The two youthful guards stumbled to their feet and to attention.

"Sir!" one said. "This man has knocked Sergeant Burrows unconscious."

"Go attend to him." Major Doyle responded in disbelief. Jesse Burrows was one of the Major's best soldiers in the youth army. Yet, this old man was able to render him unconscious. This would cause Jesse great humiliation.

Joey smiled in spite of herself.

Good for Grandfather! I'm glad he was able to teach Jesse a lesson.

"Why have you disrupted these proceedings?" The leader of the panel demanded.

"I've come to stand with my granddaughter." Grandfather announced.

"As you wish, you old fool," Major Doyle said. "I have no qualms about killing you as well. We can always use another body to grind up for food to give to the poor."

Grandfather stepped over to Joey and held out his hand. She reluctantly placed hers in it. Personal contact was strictly forbidden, yet Joey watched her hand move as if it had a mind of its own. Joey's heart raced anxiously at his touch. Her hand nearly matched his in size. The drugs Major had been forcing her to take had made her twelve year old body nearly as large as an adult's.

"That's disgusting," Major Doyle said. "Your weakness shows Benson. It is that weakness that has caused your downfall."

When the Major turned his head, Joey slipped her hand away from her grandfather's. This touching made her too uncomfortable and this was a time for clear thinking. Joey turned toward the panel and steeled herself for the trial.

"You have been charged with disobeying the orders of your commanding officer, gross misconduct on the night of the Underground raid, allowing a prisoner to escape, desertion, resisting arrest, and assault on an officer of the Militia." The clerk read.

"How do you plead?" The leader of the panel inquired.

Joey stood in stony silence. Her face displayed no emotion.

"We don't need her admission of guilt. We have seen the demonstration of her weakness before our very eyes." Major Doyle interrupted.

"The facts are clear, and we are not interested in any excuses you might conjure up." Commandant Johnson, the head of the panel, growled.

Joey shifted nervously. Drawing upon all of her training resources, she stood holding her inner thoughts in check.

"You have disgraced this New Order and your leaders." The commandant continued. "It is our opinion that we must make an example of you. We must discourage others from developing such weaknesses."

Joey became enraged at the mockery of the hearing, and the panel members' pitiful attempts to kill the Resistance movement. She hoped it would someday overthrow them, even if she would not be around to see it.

"Therefore, it is the judgement of this panel that you are to be stripped of your rank and sentenced to death. This sentence will be carried out as soon as the necessary preparations are made. Your fellow compatriots will be ordered to observe your execution, so they will learn not to test our patience. Disposing of you quickly will also prevent further infection of anyone else with your weakness."

"At the time of your execution, you will not be given any opportunity to speak. However, we will give you an opportunity to address this panel now. What, if anything, do you have to say?"

"In the light of your past record," Major Doyle interrupted, "the panel might reconsider your fate if you begged them for mercy. Perhaps, with some retraining and certain drugs, we can find some useful purpose for you. Let's see how well you can beg."

Joey remembered her earlier vow, and anger welled up in her again. Did he think her to be so weak that she would beg him or anyone else for mercy? "I won't beg you for mercy, not now, not ever!" She said through clenched teeth.

"You've got a little more spunk than I gave you credit for," he chuckled. "Pity! You had such potential."

Grandfather looked at Joey, his eyes full of pride.

"Do you have anything productive to say?" the commandant growled.

"I would like to say one more thing" -- Joey squared her shoulders, stood straight and glared at the Major -- "be sure to use bullets in the gun this time."

Major Doyle chuckled, "Don't you worry. We will have every gun loaded. We have no further need of testing your worthiness. You have already proven that you are not worthy. In fact, we have special bullets that will cause great pain and agony when they hit the flesh, creating a torturous death. It will be a pleasure to watch you die in agony. Be sure to make a good show of it will you Benson?"

Joey was determined to show her courage through her stare.

Major Doyle was the first to break the stare. He ordered, "Matthews, B., load fifteen rifles for the firing squad and have them on the parade grounds within the hour."

"Yes sir!" Bobby Matthews saluted and left the room. His twin brother, Randy had already defected and was escorting Jane Benson, Joey's grandmother, to freedom.

"I will enjoy watching you both suffer and die," the Major chuckled as he circled around Joey. "It will be a great triumph to decrease the membership of the Underground Movement by one."

Joey continued staring at the Major. She swallowed hard trying to keep her fear in check.

"Corporal Nelson, Private Martin!" Major barked.

Steve Nelson and Jerry Martin took a quick step forward. "Yes sir!" They responded in unison.

"Do you think you can handle ushering the prisoners to the parade grounds?"

"Yes sir!"

"If they give you any trouble, kill the old one, immediately, but whatever you do, keep Lieutenant Benson alive long enough to face the firing squad. Am I clear?"

"Yes sir!" Steve and Jerry saluted and ushered Joey and her grandfather out of the room, toward the parade grounds.

Upon arrival, Steve tied the prisoners' hands and stood them at the end of the field. There would be no blindfolds for them. The New Order wanted everyone to see death coming, they believed it would somehow increase the horror.

Fifteen young soldiers marched toward Joey and her grandfather. They came to a halt thirteen feet from the prisoners. Major Doyle appeared with the members of the legal panel following.

"Joey Benson, this New Order has sentenced you to death for treasonous acts against the government." Major Doyle thundered. "Because of this crime, you will receive no privileges offered to the condemned."

"I wouldn't give you the satisfaction of misconstruing my words." Joey interrupted as she stared at the armed squad before her.

"Silence!" Major Doyle ordered.

Grandfather bowed his head in prayer.

Contempt resounded in the Major's voice. "Ready!"

The squad grabbed their rifles.

Joey knew that the end was near. After all the months spent in her training, the war, watching the intense movies, and the missions, she expected to die with a more dramatic flare. The movie scenes of death by firing squad flashed through her mind.

"Aim!"

The guns were brought to firing level and the soldiers looked through their sights.

There would be no doubt regarding their aim. Every one of them was a skilled marksman. They had to be. There was no room for anything less.

"Fire!"

Joey took a deep breath and bit the inside of her lip. She braced herself at the sound of the bang. The smoke drifted to her nose. Suddenly, she realized that she was still standing.

In an instant, the bushes behind them were alive with gun fire. Joey turned around in shock. Before she could comprehend what had taken place, Bobby Matthews was behind them cutting them loose.

"Shh-hh. Don't say a word." He whispered.

"What happened?" Joey asked.

"The bullets were blanks," Bobby said. "Come with me! We've only got a few seconds more of distractions. Soon they'll realize what has taken place, and we'll all be dead."

Joey and her grandfather raced after Bobby. The Major, the panel, and the firing squad were too busy hitting the deck in the confusion.

Bobby led them back into the school building.

"Where are we going?" Joey yelled. "This isn't exactly my first choice of escape routes!"

"Will you shut up?"

"Why . . . "

"Keep your voice down! We don't want anyone to hear what direction we're running in." Bobby commanded. "I'm going to hide you in here. This is the last place they'll ever look for you. The Major will send squads combing the country side trying to recapture you. They'll search the community, the woods, and everywhere else. We wouldn't have a chance of making it to freedom. If I hide you here and wait, biding our time, we will have an easier escape later. What matters is, that for the time being, you're alive."

"Where's this hiding place that will buy us all of this time?"

"In the Major's office."

"Are you out of your mind?"

"Trust me! You're alive and safe for the time being."

113

Bobby led the way into the Major's office with Joey and her grandfather a step behind. Moving to a panel behind the Major's desk, Bobby placed his finger against a spot on the wall. The panel moved, revealing a small, closet-like space with a few water bottles placed against the wall.

"Get in there!" Bobby ordered. "Certain passages and spaces like this one were created during the remodeling. Most people don't know that they are even here. The Underground discovered these when one of the builders joined their ranks. They began using this as a means of smuggling defectors out of the area."

Joey and Henry Benson crawled into the space, Bobby replaced the panel and slipped out of the room.

Her life had been spared again, but for what purpose?

CHAPTER 13
ENEMIES AT LARGE

The lives of Joey and her grandfather had been spared, but how long could they survive? They were crammed into such a tiny space. Their bodies were protesting with cramped muscles, the call of nature, and other objections. So many questions she wished she had time to ask Bobby, but there had been no time.

Fear's icy grip held onto Joey's insides causing stabbing pains that reached up and tried to strangle her. Death certainly would be preferable to this agony or even to imprisonment.

Perhaps being shot by the firing squad would have been preferable. After all, wouldn't a quick death be better than a torturous life? One positive thing about our escape is that Grandfather's life has also been spared. He is a valuable member of the Underground and would be hard to replace. He has to lead the people to freedom. People depend upon him.

The space was dark and every creak of the floor made her heart leap. Her muscles were cramped. The air was thick, dank and hot causing sweat to run continuously down her back. Breathing was laborious. Joey was not sure if it was the air causing the difficulty breathing or the fear she felt inside.

Fate had smiled upon her and thwarted the plans of Major Doyle and the panel. Maybe that was reason enough to remain alive. She would be a continuous reminder of the New Order's failure in her programming.

Time seemed to stand still as Joey and her grandfather sat silently and motionlessly. Joey became a victim of her own thoughts.

What if it's a trick? What if this is another cruel test designed by

115

Major Doyle? How can I be sure I can trust Bobby? Does Bobby feel the same as his brother, Randy? I wonder if Grandfather is having any of these same thoughts?

They dare not risk speaking lest they betray themselves. She felt very alone.

Her mind wandered back to another such time and space. Only in this one, she was being tested and toughened. That space was probably about the same size as this one. She remembered that she could barely roll over inside of it. It was dark like this one, but Joey swore the other space contained bugs or rodents as well. During her test, fear demanded that she call out to her captors, but she dare not. Calling out would cause her to fail the test, to be tortured further and probably sent to the Pleasure Farm.

Everyone feared the Pleasure Farm. It really was not a farm, but a type of prison. Anyone that failed in the training of the New Order could be sent there. She had heard rumors that those sent there were not allowed to wear clothing and were there only for the purpose of entertaining and satisfying the military leaders. It did not matter to her if the rumors were true or not. She knew beyond a shadow of a doubt that this was a place she wanted to avoid.

Joey's mind jumped back to reality at the sound of a raspy whisper.

"Hey!" Bobby's voice was heard through the panel. "The Major and his crew are out searching for the two of you. We still will have to hurry."

Both Joey and her grandfather moved to their wobbly feet. Bobby held up his hand in protest.

"Wait! We can't get both of you through at the same time." Bobby whispered.

"Joey can go first!" Grandfather announced unselfishly.

"No!" Joey argued.

"I think it would be better for Joey to stay here. She knows their tactics, and if she's discovered, she'll have a better chance of eluding them than you would sir." Bobby informed. "With all due respect."

Grandfather finally agreed.

"I'll be back for you as soon as I can!" Bobby said. "This way Mr. Benson." He motioned.

Henry Benson squeezed Joey's shoulder, the panel was replaced, and they were gone leaving Joey alone in the dark to continue with her torturous thoughts and memories.

The hours passed unmarked in the darkness. Time hung heavy on her mind. At times she feared the blackness would just swallow her up for all eternity. Every creak of the floor caused her heart to leap. The loneliness weighed heavily on her. Joey pulled her legs closer to her chest and began to rock. Finally, evoking her training, Joey tried to plan her strategy.

The hours passed and nature called. Panic set in on Joey; she wondered what she should do?

What if someone hears me move? What if the smell creeps out?

She decided to do what she had to on one side of the space and sit on the other side. She would not be able to think about anything else if she did not. It was not long until the smell of urine mixed with the heaviness of the air nauseated her.

Her misery was interrupted by a distant voice. The crispness of it nearly frightened her into an attention stance.

"Benson must be found! I don't care how you do it, but she must be found. Her escape could mean our downfall. She knows too much. If she connects with the Underground, she could turn the common people even more against us. I want her captured, or I'll have someone's head."

Joey recognized the crisp voice as the Major's but the other voice she could not place.

"Should we commit another squadron to the search?"

"Yes, we must find Benson. Use every means available to you to find them and to find the individuals responsible for helping them escape. We must make examples of all of them."

"What if others start wavering in their loyalty?"

"Put a stop to it before it begins!" Increase the control drugs immediately for everyone. Make them mindless zombies if you have to."

"Yes sir! Is there anything else sir?"

"Bring me Private Willie King from the brig. It is time that I deal with her offense. A firm hand must be present in all areas of the New Order or we'll lose everything. Even with this Benson crisis, we must show strength."

"Yes sir!"

Joey heard the door shut and there was silence. She assumed that the Major was still on the other side of the panel.

Private Willie King is the same age as me. Rumor in the brig has it that she freaked out at a training film. Her emotional response was so great that it took a whole squadron to subdue her. I wonder what the Major is planning on doing to her.

A knock on the Major's door startled Joey back to the present.

"Enter!" Major Doyle barked.

The door opened and Joey heard a weak voice respond in what seemed to be a mumble.

"You call that an announcement?" The Major growled. "I want to hear who is requesting my attention. Now do it again and do it right!"

"Yes sir!" The voice was a little louder this time. "Private Willie King reporting as ordered."

"Still unacceptable, but it doesn't matter anymore for you. You have demonstrated your inferiority on numerous occasions. I could list the dates and incidents, but I'll spare myself the trouble. It is for this reason that you have been detained in the brig. There is no room in this New Order's military for inferiority in the ranks. I would never ask a member of the youth military to rely on someone so inferior, would you?"

"No sir!" The weak voice replied. There was no other answer to the question.

"I'm glad we're in agreement. One who is inferior is a disgrace to that uniform you are wearing . . . "

Joey gulped. She knew the next step. It was no secret. This was considered to be part of the fear tactics they used to control their youth.

"Remove the uniform! You are unfit to wear it."

"Yes sir!" The weak voice was becoming shakier.

There was silence for what seemed like an eternity. Joey felt the urge to break out of her room and rescue the Private from this horrible moment, but she could not. She would put at risk the entire Underground Resistance Movement by such an act; so she remained helpless in the darkness of her hiding place.

"The underwear is part of the uniform." Major Doyle broke the silence.

"Remove it! You are so inferior that I cannot in good consciousness allow you to hide behind clothing. You must be exposed for the inferior weakling that you are."

Another moment of silence and then Joey heard soft sobs coming from the Major's office.

"Again you demonstrate your inferiority. It is the will of the New Order that you are sentenced to the Pleasure Farm for the rest of your natural life. With that sentence, I am authorized and required to break you in."

Joey sat there in shock. She had always been too afraid to believe the rumors she had heard. Her heart began to ache until it drove her out of the safety of her hiding place.

This is wrong.

"Stop!" Joey shouted as she clumsily kicked at the panel that separated her from the Major. She had not anticipated her sleeping muscles to be so awkward.

The panel gave way, she stumbled out and there she sat face to face with Major Doyle and the small naked girl.

CHAPTER 14
THE FEAR GAME

In that instant, Joey knew she had let the Underground Movement down and had disappointed everyone who had risked their lives to rescue her. Yet, what the Major was about to do to that young girl was wrong. She was not sure why she thought it was wrong or who said it was wrong. All the propaganda and training she received promoted such a thing as part of their training, but something deep inside of her thrust her into action. She feared this action would now cost her dearly.

"Well, if it isn't Benson!...Very Clever!" The Major said as he checked his clothing to regain his intimidating appearance. "I have every soldier in this sector out searching for you and that little band of degenerates that are disrupting the land; and here you are; right under my nose; waiting to slip away when we tire of the chase."

Joey finally got the blood circulating in her legs and was able to struggle to a wobbly stand.

"You know what's wrong with you Benson? You developed a heart somewhere along the way. I don't know how or why. If given the opportunity, perhaps our scientists would find you an interesting case study. But, the opportunity will not present itself. There is absolutely no room in this New Order for a heart."

Joey's mind raced as she tried to establish her options. She was unarmed and not quite sure where Willie King's loyalties were at this point. One thing was for certain, she had to take some type of action now and therefore have to take her chances.

Joey lunged toward the Major's desk. That act of surprise allowed Joey to grab the Major's sidearm he had placed on the desk. She wasted no time aiming it.

"I'm not afraid to use this Major." Joey announced. "And thanks to you, I qualify as a marksman."

The Major appeared unshaken by her action. He almost seemed amused. "What do you think you're going to do now? You can't escape from here." He spoke casually as he moved toward his desk and sat in his chair, without talking his eyes off of Joey.

"Big mistake letting your heart guide you. You probably could have stayed held up in your little hole there until your friends came for you."

She inched her way clear of the Major's reach. Joey needed to be very careful and not dare drop her guard. Major Doyle was known to be extremely tricky.

"Grab your clothes!" Joey ordered the girl assuming that the Private would join her. Private King did as Joey ordered.

Turning her attention back to Major Doyle. "And don't touch that desk Major! I know you have either a weapon or perhaps some way to summon your guards there."

Suddenly, Private King tossed her boots at Joey distracting her long enough for Major Doyle to jump to his feet and snatch the gun.

Joey looked dumbfounded at the girl. "Why?" She managed.

Private King straightened herself to attention and replied, "I had a chance to prove that I am still worthy to be an active member of this New Order. It seemed more logical to defend the New Order and to be loyal to my oath, which is something you seem to have forgotten. You had a place of safety and you betrayed yourself for me - a stranger. What a fool you are!"

Joey gaped.

Major Doyle laughed at the expression on Joey Benson's face. Walking over to his desk, he pushed a button on his desk and instantly two guards appeared, fully armed.

"Take Private King back to the brig while I contemplate her actions during this crisis. Perhaps the merit of this action may outweigh her previous offenses."

"Yes sir!"

The two security guards took the naked private back to the brig. Joey thought she had detected a faint smile on the face of Private King.

But what did it matter. How stupid can I be? I've ruined everything and for what? How could I have misjudged the power of the New Order on an individual?

She was alone and in the hands of the New Order's Militia. No one even knew she was in trouble. She had betrayed the members of the Underground. To make things worse, she was standing face-to-face with Major Doyle. Sitting at his desk, he leaned way back in his chair and stared at her. Joey shifted nervously. She tried to hold onto all of the training lest he have the satisfaction of breaking her.

"What shall we do with the former Lieutenant Joey Benson?" He paused a moment. "The only answer I come up with is what we already decided, to make you an example. Doing this will create fear within the ranks even more than there has ever been before. After all, it is fear that keeps everyone in their place. I especially enjoy the power that wields the fear." Major Doyle paused a moment to scrutinize her. "Yes, that is what we will do."

Speaking as if he were speaking only to himself. "We will make an example of you to the entire population." He decided. "Then we will use this fear we create to force the people to surrender any Underground members they know. The Underground will no doubt try to rescue you once again. Fools that they are! That rescue attempt will be their downfall." He laughed aloud sounding quite pleased with his brilliance.

"Yes, you are our trophy. You will be the instrument that will bring about the downfall of the Underground." His laugh sounded so evil that it made Joey shudder inside.

"It was wrong of us to condemn you to die immediately. Letting you live for a while as an example to those, who would rebel against this New Order would be more profitable, and so much more pleasurable. Killing you would be too quick a punishment. We will draw it out and make you beg us to end your miserable existence."

Joey tuned out the Major's ravings. She had let everyone down and that was torturous enough. Now others would suffer because of her stupidity. She would be used by the New Order to do more damage than she had done

in all of the days that she commanded. She would become part of their training an example of what not to do.

*Why did I pay attention to anything but my programming? I'm just a
pawn in this great game of fear.*

CHAPTER 15
REIGN OF TERROR

The Major pushed the button on his desk again and the two security guards reappeared in their methodical way.

"Get the training cuffs! We don't want her escaping again."

One guard disappeared and returned moments later holding the training cuffs in his hand. These were specially designed handcuffs that had bits of metal that would push into the skin of the wearer's hands, causing agonizing pain as the bits pressed into the flesh of the wrists. As long as the person did not struggle against them, they did not draw blood. Their purpose was to train an individual to endure intense pain for long periods of time.

"Chain Benson securely! She will be traveling at my side while we tour the neighboring communities. I want her to see every moment of the reign of terror that she caused by her escape."

"Yes sir!"

The two guards hastened to obey the Major's orders.

"Keep your eye on her! She's a sly one."

One guard leveled his weapon at her while the other busied himself with the chains.

Joey felt the metal bite into her wrist. She bit her tongue to prevent any visible reaction. Her training shouted instructions to her brain.

"Since you seem to have developed a heart, we will let your heart be the instrument of your punishment. I warned you about hearts being a source of torture, and now you will understand my words fully."

"Ready sir!" The guard reported.

Joey's hands were cuffed in front of her with a chain around her waist holding them securely at her waist.

"Very well!" The Major said after inspecting the restraints for himself. He gave the training cuffs a quick yank. Pain coursed through her arms. Clenching her teeth forced the rising scream back inside of her to be silent. He did not want any surprises like the one on the parade grounds. "Get my car!"

One of the security guards saluted and exited the room.

Once in the car, they began driving around the neighborhoods that surrounded the former school building now converted to the military complex. Every place Joey turned, she saw destruction caused by those who were searching for her.

There were road blocks where the young soldiers were stopping cars and physically pulling the occupants from their vehicles and beating them to their knees. Others searched vehicles to the point of destroying them.

Joey hoped that Bobby was able to get her grandfather to safety. In another direction, Joey noticed plumes of smoke climbing into the air. This acrid smoke hung over some of the homes. She saw people trying desperately to save their few belongings allotted to them by the Republic, while others used pails and other containers to try and prevent the fire from spreading. All the while, the young soldiers stood by watching and laughing at the havoc they created. These super-soldiers were destroying the homes and property of their own parents and other relatives.

Joey observed a man standing by what used to be the door of the smoldering ruins of his home. The man had tears coursing down his face, and she could hear him wailing at his loss. He had lost everything. Sharp pains filled her chest. Joey did not know their cause or why her throat ached. She only knew she had been the spark that began this devastation.

What would they do now? No shelter, no belongings, nothing. It's all my fault.

Joey knew the area's fragile economy could not afford such total disruption and devastation.

"Think of this as a cleansing fire, Benson. This will cleanse this area of the disease laden Underground. If they had let us execute you and that old man, perhaps their belongings and lives would have been spared."

The pains became more intense as the Major's words sunk deep into her soul.

Why did his words cause her so much pain? Wasn't she supposed to be immune to pain?

"If you have names of those that came to your aid or others that may be in the Underground, we can put a stop to some of this."

"I don't know anything!" Her words were thick as she fought desperately against her rioting emotions.

"Pity! I guess our reign of terror must continue as we search for those Underground members. We will find them. The only question that remains is how much destruction and death must occur first."

Joey looked away from the fires. She was already responsible for destroying a major hiding place for defectors, now this. Both the Underground members and innocent people within the New Order are paying the price for her lack of judgment. Strength seemed to drain out of her, yet the pain inside of her increased. This pain seemed as though it would consume her. All of her training never prepared her for pain of this magnitude. She felt as if her insides would eat her alive.

The Major was watching her with a great deal of interest. He was waiting for some weakness to show itself, so he could exploit it.

She needed to be careful not to telegraph her misery. He would find it too enjoyable.

"I see you are withstanding the pain nobly, but this is only the beginning of your pain Benson." Major Doyle said. "Driver, return to base!"

"Soon you will see the slow, torturous death of those who dare to facilitate your rescue."

The Major paused for a moment and then continued.

"You know Benson, I'm really puzzled about this decision you've made to turn against us. Before the Militia took you in, you were worthless. We gave you your identity. We made you the strong individual that you were. Why would you want to throw all of that away?" He paused as if waiting for an answer.

Joey swallowed hard trying to lessen the inner pain. Death would definitely be more preferable than this pain.

I can handle the physical pain, but it's this inside pain that I'm not sure about.

Joey knew she must endure! She must survive in order to tell others of the New Order's plan. She must survive until she could make amends for the problems she caused. More important, she had to survive to spite Major Doyle and the other leaders. It would be her indomitable spirit and those like her that would rise above the New Order's military rule and eventually restore their world to a more peaceful existence.

CHAPTER 16
TORTURED EXISTENCE

The security guards escorted Joey to a room known as the inner office. This room had been nicknamed by the youth army as the "chamber of horrors". She would have the opportunity to learn first hand if the rumors were exaggerated, or if they only began to touch the surface of what was really there.

Joey glanced around the room anxiously. The room was almost barren. It had no windows and only the one visible door. She could discern two chairs and a desk in the dim light. Nothing in the room gave her any indication of what fate awaited her.

"Exchange the training cuffs for handcuffs." Major Doyle ordered.

The security guards quickly obeyed.

As the bite of the training cuffs fell away, Joey felt a wave of relief flow through her body. The guard quickly replaced them with regular handcuffs, but she still felt a relief.

"Lower the tether!"

"Yes sir!"

Joey's attention was diverted to a cable with some sort of locking device being lowered from the ceiling. She had not heard any rumors about what was the cable's purpose, but she was sure it was not anything she would enjoy.

The other guard kept his eyes fixed on the Major, waiting for the Major's command.

The Major signaled the guard. He grabbed Joey and shoved her into position under the descending cable. The guard connected the cable to the cuffs on Joey's hands. When the Major nodded, the second guard reversed the switch and the cable began retracting. Joey felt her hands being raised involuntarily toward the ceiling. Slowly they were pulled over her head until her arms were fully stretched. Still the cable retracted. As the cable continued, Joey's feet began lifting off of the floor. The Major signaled the guard, and the cable came to a halt. If Joey stood on her toes, she could ease the strain on her arms.

"Does it hurt?" Major Doyle taunted.

Joey glared in silence.

"Good! At least you still remember the correct answer."

"Now Benson, you will experience some things first hand that you and your compatriots have only seen in training films. The resistance that we painstakingly built into you through the drugs, the indoctrination, and all of the other elements that made up your training will not keep you from breaking under the weight of reality." He motioned toward the cable. "...when you develop a heart." He finished his previous thought. "I will break you down and expose you as the inferior being that you have proven yourself to be. I will show everyone what happens to anyone who dares to rebel against this New Order. Once we have broken you down, we will be able to use your failure to completely destroy the Underground Resistance."

I vowed before, and I vow again, he will never break me down.

Major Doyle seemed intoxicated at his own words. The guard nearer to her was floating on the Major's every word. Joey managed to pull her body up and landed a kick to the side of the guard's head.

"Still have some fight left in you," the Major chuckled. "We'll see how long it will last."

He began walking toward the door.

"I will leave you alone to become better acquainted with your pain." With those words, Major Doyle left the room yelling at the guard for his inattention.

The pain in her arms slowly became excruciating. Her only relief came when she stood on her toes, but even that grew tiring. Before long, pain engulfed her entire body.

The time alone allowed Joey the opportunity to rest her defenses to some degree. Constant bombardment of her senses could cause them to break if she did not allow them to have an occasional respite.

Pain does funny things to one's mind. Somewhere in the foggy shadows of her mind, Joey saw a little girl with curly brown hair running and laughing through a field. An elderly man was holding out his hands for her to come to him. With a scoop of his arms, she was next to him ... suddenly soldiers were wrestling the girl from the man's hands and dragging her away.

"No!" The sound of her voice echoing off the walls startled her. Immediately her mind responded to the reality of the pain and the loneliness of the room.

Unsure of the amount of time that had passed, Joey cursed herself for allowing her mind to wander. Now she felt disoriented and that was a bad thing. If she wanted to remain strong, she needed to stay focused. With great effort, she fought back the fog of confusion.

Suddenly, the room brightened. Joey squinted, forcing her eyes to focus. She had to see everything that was happening in the room. She wanted no surprises. Her survival depended being prepared.

"How are we doing?" Major Doyle said in a voice that seemed to be almost cheerful.

Major Doyle took a seat behind the desk and poured himself a glass of water.

Joey's mouth was dry and her throat ached from thirst. She longed for a sip of water.

You're not fooling me. That's one of the first lessons we learned about breaking down prisoners. This was a lesson I passed with flying colors. How stupid does he think I am?

Her attention was uncontrollably drawn back to the glass of the water.

"Would you like some?"

Joey tried to ignore him.

Why is he using the basic tricks?

"You want to know what the catch is, right?" He paused a moment. "No catch, really!" Pausing a moment, he continued. "Well, maybe one little one, you give me the names I want. I give you some water - Simple! One name - one sip of water."

Joey clenched her jaw and concentrated on survival.

"No, huh! Not ready to give in?"

A knock on the door and a guard entered bringing the Major his breakfast.

Her attention was once more drawn uncontrollably to the desk.

"Maybe food will be the straw that weakens you. Hungry?...Same deal as the water."

The smell of the food made her stomach growl. She could not remember when she had eaten last.

Three days, maybe four.

Major Doyle took his time eating his breakfast. Every mouthful was exaggerated. When he finished, he summoned the guard. This time two guards entered the room. One took the Major's dishes while the other one stood behind Joey. The Major nodded and the guard cupped one fist inside of the other, and swung his arms, striking Joey in the small of the back.

A scream of agony escaped her lips as the guard's fists struck aching body. The force of the blow caused her to swing on the cable. The stress on her joints sent new waves of pain throughout her body.

"Funny how you think your pain tolerance has peaked and you couldn't possibly hurt any more. Then something happens, and a whole new generation of pain rolls through," the Major laughed. "Soon you will give me the information I want. You're not as strong as you think you are."

Finally, Joey managed to stop the swinging by catching her toes on the floor to stop herself. A wave of relief covered her. The smallest things could make a big difference.

The Major chuckled as he left the room.

I wish I were not the source of his entertainment.

Joey was left alone again in her misery. Time dragged on with no meaning. Day or night; lunch or dinner; they all rolled into the same isolated, torturous moment. Disorientation continued to threaten her. Joey searched her mind for some solitude where she could retreat and find some mental relief.

Some time later, Major Doyle returned. It seemed quicker than before, maybe that was a distortion of reality, or maybe it really was only a short period of time. Joey knew many of the ploys the New Order used to break someone down. The leadership had trained them well. Each had experienced these things during their training, but with less intensity. To confuse one regarding time was one of the most successful ploys. Changing the concept of time forced the victim's mind to attack him. When that occurred, their demise was only a matter of time.

The Major entered the room, followed by the two guards. Joey steeled herself for another blow. Preparation was the key to survival. The blow did not come. Instead, a guard crossed the room to the switch for the cable and began to lower it. As her feet fully touched the ground, her legs gave way under her. The second guard crossed over to Joey and unlocked the handcuffs, freeing her from the tether. She toppled to the floor. The guards exited the room, leaving her alone with Major Doyle. He seated himself behind the desk.

What is he planning? I've got to be ready.

Joey rubbed her arms trying to get the circulation moving again. She kept her eyes fixed on Major Doyle. Moments later the guards returned carrying two plates of food and a bottle of water. He motioned for Joey to come sit in the chair near his desk.

Why was he doing this? This a trick? What should I do? Should I go over there or remain here on the floor?

While she was contemplating the Major's sudden change of disposition, he motioned for the guards. Joey braced herself.

With one swoop, they picked her up and deposited her in the chair near the desk.

Alarms were going off in her head. *This is a trick!*

The rush of blood through her body made her dizzy and unable to think clearly.

The Major poured her a glass of water.

"Drink?"

Her mouth was beyond dry. She could not muster enough spit to even coat the inside of her mouth.

Major Doyle offered her the cup of water again.

He didn't mention any strings attached this time. Why was he now being so humane? What will the water cost me? Is it a price that I can pay?

She craved the water. Thirst forced her to throw caution aside for the moment and reach for the cup. Her fingers were still too stiff to grasp the cup. Forcing her hands together by a conscious act of her will, she managed to wedge the cup between them. The water sloshed over her mouth and down her face, yet her tongue managed to trap a few drops and pull them into her mouth.

The water felt good in her dry mouth. Her suspicions about the Major returned.

Why would he now be almost kind to me? Surely nothing has changed.

Major Doyle leaned back in his chair studying her every movement. She felt self-conscious. A look of pleasure came over his face as she squirmed in spite of herself.

Joey's instincts cautioned her not to relax around him.

Don't trust him! This is a trick! Stay alert!

Her body was so fatigued and sore. She was having a hard time fighting the fatigue.

Soon Joey's muscles started to loosen from the knots they had tied themselves into earlier. At that moment, Major Doyle jumped forward and slapped Joey so hard, she flew out of the chair and crashed to the floor.

Joey fell in a crumpled heap. The taste of the blood coated the inside of her mouth. Her training ordered her to get up, but her body dictated a different message. Ignoring the pain, Joey struggled to her feet.

Major Doyle laughed. "Your instincts have not been too corrupted yet by this heart of yours." Then he struck her again. The force of the blow knocked her backwards to the floor, knocking her breath out. Panic filled her mind. Gasping for air but none came. The room grew dark.

Am I dying?

When she awoke, confusion had settled into her brain. The flow of air once again filled her lungs. She should have guessed that Major Doyle was preparing to trick her by his kindness.

Why are my instincts wavering?

Too weak to force her body up, Joey remained on the floor. She could not see Major Doyle. Joey believed that he must have exited the room. Drifting in and out of consciousness, she did not know how long she lay on the floor. During one of her more lucid moments, Joey noticed a guard slipping into the room. It was a guard she had not seen here before.

The guard cautiously entered the room, closing the door quietly behind him. Crossing the room to Joey, he leaned over her. She braced herself for further punishment. Punishing a prisoner by their own volition was common and even encouraged by the Militia.

"C'mon, I'm getting you out of here." The guard said as he attempted to pull her to her feet.

"No!" Joey was leery of trusting another person after what happened with the Major. She took an awkward swing at the guard causing her to fall back to the floor.

"I'm from the Underground. My orders are to get you out of here before Major Doyle can make you their national symbol."

"No!" Joey shouted. She tried to wrestle away from the guard.

"Will you shut up?" The guard hissed as he tried to pick her up again.

"You want me to trust you, so you can have pleasure in inflicting more pain. What kind of a fool do you think I am?" Joey mumbled and swung at him again.

"I don't have time for this." In desperation, he pulled out a hypo and sedated her..

CHAPTER 17
HUNT FOR REVENGE

Joey worked at forcing her eyes open, but they were too heavy. Perhaps keeping them closed would make the pain that blanketed her body go away.

Where am I? Where is the Major?... her thoughts wandered.

Voices faded in and out as Joey tried to push the fog from her brain. She needed to focus.

"That robot of the New Order has already caused the compromise of one very important escape route. Do you know what this alone will cost us in human lives? Why would you want to take another chance on her? Just let Major Doyle kill her."

"She's not a robot! She has the potential of being converted back to normal."

"Normal! That's a laugh. There is no normal for them, between the drugs and the brainwashing, they forever belong to the New Order heart, mind, and soul."

Joey could not identify the voices. Her eyes still refused to open. She desperately wanted to see the faces of those who were talking about her in such a manner.

I'll have them all killed for such insults.

"I'm sure there's a logical reason for what she did."

"Good reason or not, I'm not willing to take a chance at compromising our entire Underground Resistance Movement for the salvation of one; especially when that kid is the most highly decorated and respected kid under that demon's command. I am still of the old school that believes "the needs of the many still outweigh the needs of the few." In case you haven't figured it out, *we* are the many in this scenario."

"Perhaps your axiom is correct, but this kid is the granddaughter of one of our founders. We have to do all we can to move her to safety and pray that our kindness will not be betrayed again. We owe it to her grandfather."

Joey unable to maintain her level of consciousness, let the voices fade into the fog of her brain. When she awoke later, her eyes were finally able to open. Focusing was another issue. Her eyes were blurred. She could not discern the objects in the room.

Where am I? Last thing I remember, I was in Major Doyle's torture chamber and that strange guard was there . . .

Her thoughts were interrupted by one of the voices she remembered hearing in the fog.

"Well, look who's awake!"

Joey turned toward the voice with an apprehensive look.

"Hi! My name is Rachel Lewis. I'm sorry this was not the most hospitable way to get you to our place for a visit. Also, I'm sorry our we had to drug you, but your lack of cooperation was costing us valuable time. We had to get you out of there any way we could."

Rachel Lewis appeared to be eighteen or nineteen. She had medium length blonde hair, and was very tall. Her smile puzzled Joey. People under the command of the New Order do not smile unless they are inflicting pain on another.

Joey stared at Rachel trying to comprehend her words. Her disorientation was evident.

"You look puzzled. I'll be glad to answer any questions you may have," she said cheerfully.

Joey could not force her thoughts down to her mouth, so she remained silent.

"I know you have questions. Let's see if I can provide answers to the questions in your head. You are in an undisclosed location controlled by the Underground Resistance Movement. We rescued you from the Major's torture chamber."

Rachel put her hand out to touch Joey's shoulder, but Joey recoiled in fear. There was no comfort in another's touch for her.

"I'm sorry, I should have realized. . . .It's okay!" Rachel tried to sound comforting. "We've had several young people that were products of the New

Order pass through our doors. We know that you'll find it hard to trust us, and that's okay. We can be patient. I hope we can convince you that we understand!"

Joey still stared at the pleasant face that sat in front of her, trying to comprehend what she was saying.

"I brought you some broth! Take it! You've been through a lot. You'll need to rebuild your strength, but it will take a little time. I don't know the extent of the torture that you've been through. I'm afraid that your body will recover much faster than your emotions."

Joey remembered the situation with the water that Major Doyle had tricked her with. Her stomach growled at the smell of the broth.

Sensing her uneasiness, Rachel announced, "I'll leave you with the broth. Perhaps you'll take it if I leave. There's a straw in it so you don't need to try and grasp the cup."

Rachel placed the cup of broth with the straw on the table that crossed the bed that Joey was lying in.

"Shall I help you to sit up?"

Joey shook her head.

With that Rachel left.

Joey's eyes darted around the room looking for a trap or some sort of secret camera. She did not want to be on display or be used in some cruel form of entertainment.

Convinced that there was no one waiting in the wings to attack her, she struggled to raise herself into a seated position. Her arms and legs felt very weak and for a moment refused to respond to her brain, but her will finally conquered her physical body. With sheer determination, Joey pushed herself into a seated position and pulled the table toward her until her mouth could reach the straw.

The broth felt warm and comforting going down her throat. It seemed that a sensation of new life coursed through her arms and legs. It made her feel somewhat better. Lying her head back against the wall, Joey dozed into a troubled sleep. Her mind replayed pictures of the past:

...*body parts, torture, the firing squad* . . .

Joey jerked awake. She could hear voices again, but they were too far away for her to understand them clearly. Moments later, Rachel entered the room.

"How are you doing?" Rachel spoke as she entered the room.

Joey stared at her in silence.

"It's okay. You can talk to me! I won't hurt you. I promise!"

Promises mean nothing. Joey eyed Rachel suspiciously.

"We only want to help you."

Joey kept a stony silence.

"Well, I guess I'll let you rest some more and then perhaps you'll feel more like talking," Rachel said as she rose to her feet. "I wasn't sure when I was going to tell you this, but perhaps it will help you to talk when I return. I know some of what you've experienced. I was once a member of the youth army. I was taken from my parents, but managed to escape after about a month of their training." Rachel turned and walked out of the room.

This time, Joey remained awake. Rachel's words rolled over and over in her mind.

How could anyone escape from the Major's grasp? Why haven't we heard about this, even in rumors? Perhaps she is lying to me, so that I'll trust her.

Her eyes darted around the room looking for a means of escape or possible traps.

In the hallway an unfamiliar voice asked, "Have you told her?"

Joey's ears perked up. She knew eavesdropping was wrong, but gathering information to use as a means of escape was quite another story.

Who can be trusted? Rachel? She certainly does not look like a member of the youth army. Not to mention, members of the youth army have only one goal -- to get ahead. Is this really an Underground hiding place? Perhaps this is just another one of the Major's elaborate traps.

"What am I supposed to tell her exactly?" Rachel's voice answered.

"Major Doyle has ordered Sergeant Jesse Burrows and leading a patrol out to search for her. Rumor has it, he is hunting for her with a vengeance."

So Jesse is after me again! Joey panicked.

Jesse is a true robot of the New Order. He was and is ruthless and thrives on torturing others. It was Jesse that caused the situation that put me on this road - nearly costing the life of Grandfather. I have to escape.

Even if this was friendly territory, with Jesse Burrows hunting for her, safety was only an illusion. Her presence would endanger everyone. It would be better if she got away, found her bearings, and headed for freedom. At least if she had to face Jesse, she could face him in the open rather than being easy prey in a cage.

"No! I just don't think it would be a good idea to tell her right now. Let's wait until she regains a little strength. She's liable to try to escape when she hears the news. There's no telling what she'll do if she knew that Jesse Burrows is hunting for her."

Joey tuned out the rest of the conversation. What she needed was a plan! First order of business - get out of this bed. Joey's every movement caused her excruciating pain, a result of Major Doyle's chamber of horrors.

Joey wrestled herself to the edge of the bed. After all the effort to get up, her legs refused to stand. She fell to the floor sending new pain throughout her body.

Rachel came running into the room as soon as Joey hit the floor.

"What happened? What did you think you were doing trying to get out of bed?" Rachel said in an anxious voice. She stooped over Joey. "Are you all right?"

"Leave me alone!" Joey weakly pushed at her. "I've got to get out of here." Joey growled. Rachel seized Joey's arms and lifted the struggling Joey back into bed.

"Don't touch me!"

"I wouldn't need to touch you, if you stayed in bed."

Joey grunted.

"Now stay here! I assure you that you are in a safe place. Can you reach past your programming for one minute and listen to me? You don't need to get out of here! We won't hurt you."

Joey's expression was filled with terror. "Leave me alone!"

"You've got to let go of the New Order's hold on you. Try to find the person you were before this all happened."

"You don't know anything. You could let go of yours because you were only there a month. I've been in long enough for my entire identity to be erased. I only have the programming left. If I let go, I'll be lost. The training is designed to consume the individual, if a person doesn't follow it. There's no way around it. If you truly saw other members of the New Order, you should know that refusing the programming is not an easy solution. The Major and those like him did their job, and they did it well. There's not enough left of that other person to salvage anymore. I have to live with the results of this for the rest of my life. What you don't know, or may have forgotten is that they programmed a self-destruct button inside all of us. It's only a matter of time until the bomb goes off. While we wait, I need to stay one step ahead of them so they don't have the pleasure of winning. Don't you understand? I'm at war! War with them, and war with me."

Rachel stood in shock. She had no response. Her mouth tried to move, but she was speechless. Finally, changing the subject enabled her to find words, "Stay in bed! You're not well! You need time to regain your strength and then we'll discuss the next step."

"No! I can't stay!" Joey protested but the little strength she had mustered had been used up, and she was unable to move. "Don't you understand? My staying here endangers everyone. Jesse Burrows will kill everyone in his search for me. He is consumed by hatred, and he is completely one of their robots."

"How do you know about Jesse Burrows?" Rachel asked in surprise.

"I make it my business to know things."

"Jesse won't be coming here to look for you."

"You don't know Jesse! Do you?"

"No!"

"Well, I do! Worst of all, he knows me, and he's not very fond of me. He will hunt for me with revenge as his fuel."

"I think you can relax. I assure you. Jesse won't be looking for you here."

"Just where is here? What's so special about this place that Jesse won't come here? Major Doyle has spies everywhere. Just like you have spies within the New Order, they have infiltrators among the Underground. It doesn't matter if you think your people are trustworthy or not. Your people may have even been beaten by members of the New Order, but they could still be spies. Major Doyle has people playing all sorts of roles."

Rachel slumped to a nearby chair.

"You think you're the only ones with spies -- how stupid you are!" Joey turned her face away from Rachel.

Sensing the conversation to be over, Rachel left the room.

Joey dozed but awoke to loud shouts. She could not distinguish what the yelling was all about, but she could sense panic in the air. Sheer determination forced her body out of bed and to her feet.

Staggering toward the door, using the wall as her support, Joey approached the door. The shouts became louder and clearer.

"Code red! Code red!" A frantic voice shouted.

Code red? What do they mean by code red? Joey tried to make sense of what was happening. *No code red is ever good.*

Dizziness swam over her. She wondered if she still had some residual effects of the drugs they used to rescue her out of the Major's grasp.

She shook her head trying to clear the dizziness. *Code red must mean that something is wrong.*

"Security breech! Security breech!" Another frantic voice sounded.

Deep inside, Joey knew what it meant. Jesse and his unit had breached this Underground hold.

Why wouldn't they listen to me? There's no such thing as a safe place when it comes to Jesse Burrows. I've got to get out of here!

Joey turned and started making her way toward the window. There had to be another way out of this room. Hobbling across the floor, she felt a cold chill run down her back. Without turning around, she knew Jesse was standing behind her.

"Well, if it isn't Benson!"

Joey turned around and stood face to face with evil personified.

"You left the Major's inner chamber and didn't even stop to say goodbye. How rude!" Jesse smirked. "You look in really bad shape, but you'll look a lot worse by the time I finish with you."

"I might have something to say about that," Joey said through gritted teeth. She clenched her teeth invoking her strength of will. This would be her only chance of survival.

"Benson, even on a good day you wouldn't be able to tangle with me, so

143

don't try to make me angry. You know how I can get when I'm angry. My orders may be to bring you back alive, but I can make you beg me to let you die and still fulfill my orders." Jesse took a leisurely step toward Joey. "Oh don't think your little group of dissidents will come rescue you again. My people are keeping them very busy. It's just you and me; so let's see what you got left if you're game." Jesse took another leisurely step toward Joey, then arched his body, trying to taunt Joey into an attack formation.

"You're as yellow as they come."

Joey took a deep breath and tried to force her brain into the familiar patterns that she knew so well from her training.

"I've been waiting a long time for this, Benson. No one's going to stop me from hurting you and hurting you badly." Jesse seemed to be drunk with excitement.

Jesse lunged at her. Her body was sluggish and didn't respond as quickly as her mind ordered. Jesse spun and knocked Joey to the ground with a kick to the head. Jesse started punching wildly. Covering her head with her arms, Joey tried to protect her head and other vital organs. In this condition, she was no match for him. Her only alternative was to protect herself from serious injury. Abruptly, the pounding ceased, and Jesse's body fell over hers and didn't move. Confused, she struggled to free herself from the dead weight that was resting upon her.

Joey looked up and saw Rachel standing nearby with a hypo in her hand.

CHAPTER 18
CLOSE ENCOUNTERS

"Is he dead?" Joey finally found some words to break the silence.

"No, but he'll have one whale of a headache when he comes too - Not to mention he'll probably be very angry." Rachel said matter-of-factly.

"Kill him!" Joey ordered.

"No! I can't do that." Rachel replied with a look of shock.

"You don't understand what kind of a person you're dealing with here. You underestimated the fact that he could find you. Don't make the same mistake twice! Kill him now! If you don't kill him, he will keep on coming." Joey screamed.

"I am sworn by my oath to the Creator in Heaven not to take the life of one that He created and even he qualifies as that."

"Jesse Burrows wasn't created by your Creator. He's a product of the New Order's Militia. Perhaps you think by rendering him unconscious and moving me and your little group to another location will make everything all better. Don't you realize this is far from over?" Joey forced herself to her knees.

"Here let me help you up!" Rachel offered as she stepped toward Joey in an attempt to change the subject.

"I told you before, and I'm telling you now - leave me alone! I don't need your help. I can make it to freedom on my own. You go ahead and continue being naive. You and your little friends will all end up dead. I'm not sticking around to watch it happen." Joey shouted.

Joey struggled to her feet. Using the wall as a brace, she stood there staring at Jesse's body on the floor, and Rachel standing over it.

"We want to help you leave the New Order. We want to reunite you with your grandparents."

"I'm a liability to you and everyone else that comes in contact with me.

145

The New Order wants me back because I know too much. If they have me, they have a precious trophy they can parade around in humiliation. They will hunt you down in order to find me and destroy everything in the process. I am a pawn in their war for dominance and power. You should know these things if you were truly one of us at one time."

"You're staying with us and that's final . . . We owe that much to your grandfather for the start he gave us. It is our duty to deliver you safely to your grandparents. Besides, I didn't want to tell you this, but if you try to leave here alone our people will kill you on sight."

Joey looked at her in confusion.

"There are some here who feel you can't be trusted. Especially since you gave away one of our main hiding places."

Horror filled Joey's face. "I had good reason for what I did! Is that the reason they don't trust me?"

Rachel shook her head.

"Why?" Joey demanded.

"We've wasted enough time. We're getting out of here--NOW!" Rachel crossed over to Joey.

Joey snapped into a fighting position and just as suddenly fell to the floor with a thud.

Rachel hurried over to Joey. Bending over her, Joey immediately sat up and wrestled Rachel to the floor. Grabbing Rachel's arm, she twisted it behind her.

"It's amazing how strong one can become when they push their will and self-discipline behind it." Joey said. "I'll break your arm if you don't cooperate. I'm sorry things have to be this way, but my first responsibility is to escape. Perhaps you have forgotten that rule, but I haven't. Now come with me. Your people won't kill me as long as you are with me."

Joey was able to get to her feet without too much difficulty. She pushed Rachel ahead of her. "You convince everyone we meet all is well and they are to leave us alone."

Rachel nodded.

She pushed Rachel through the corridors. Each step made her feel a little stronger. She was not sure if she really was feeling better or if it was the adrenalin strengthening her will.

"Which way?" Joey hissed.

Rachel motioned toward the exit.

A few of the dissidents followed them at a distance. Somehow they had managed to neutralize all of Jesse's forces.

That's rather unbelievable!

"Anyone follows us, she's dead!" Joey shouted to them.

"Stop this now, and we can all walk away from it." Rachel said, trying to sound calm. "If you do this, the Underground will not be there to bail you out next time."

"There may not be a next time.... I am doing my duty."

"Can you really afford to have two enemies?"

"Can you shut your mouth for a while?"

Joey moved outside of the door pushing Rachel ahead of her. Looking in all directions, Joey saw the woods in the distance. She decided to head for them. She pulled Rachel along.

"You know you're wrong about what you said earlier." Rachel said as Joey dragged her toward the woods.

"What are you talking about?"

"You said there wasn't enough left of the person you were to salvage. You're wrong! You have to grab hold of that hope that someone will find that person. Seize onto that thread of humanity which can pull you back into a normal life! Find that hope! The New Order's programming was not flaw-less. You will eventually find someone who cares enough to lift you from this self imprisonment. You can come back from this! You can find the truth! Just the same as I did."

"Shut up! You don't know what you're talking about. No one knows the truth about what the New Order does to its youth. Anyone - especially the

New Order - can manufacture truth on an assembly line."

Joey knew that dragging a hostage along for a prolonged period of time would be detrimental. It would only slow her down and without a weapon it would be even more difficult to keep a hostage.

Joey forced Rachel to the ground.

"If you know what's good for you, you won't get up." Joey ran off deeper into the woods.

She was feeling even stronger now, almost as good as new. It was a dreary day as Joey hurried along the grassy path toward what she believed to be safety. The trees swayed slightly as a cool breeze stirred their beautiful green leaves. The sun was struggling with the clouds to shine forth, but she hoped the clouds would win.

Wandering along the path, she tried to anticipate what her next move should be. There were two groups after her now. Suddenly a deer ran across her path, causing her heart to nearly leap out of her chest. The deer scampered away and was swallowed by the darkness of the forest. She wished she could move that way and disappear like it did.

Joey hurried through the forest following the animal. She was forced to follow the trail through the woods because the forest was too thick to go off of it. The trail was narrow. A bird began to sing somewhere in a tree above her. Joey stopped walking and looked around. She wanted to be sure it really was a bird or if it was some type of signal.

The forest grew thicker, the trees and overgrowth blocked out the few last remaining strains of light. Darkness surrounded her making her feel alone and uneasy. The density of the woods caused her heart to beat faster. Yet, the serenity of the surroundings battled back with a calming effect. Joey had not been this far into the forest before. Their military training kept them closer to the main base.

A blast shattered the harmony of the woods. She jumped and looked around searching her surroundings for the source of the sound. A second blast thundered through the silence. Fear gripped her insides and ripped at her guts. Shouts followed the second blast.

Joey began running. The dust of the trail clogged her nose and throat. Her feet were moving so fast, she could barely feel the ground beneath them.

A rock rose up occasionally causing her to stumble from time to time. She had to remain free. If she were captured by Jesse and his bunch, she would be paraded back to the New Order as a trophy. If she were taken by Rachel and her people, she would endanger everyone. Not to mention, after what she just pulled, they might shoot her on sight. There would be time to contemplate her fate at a later time, now she must remain single-minded. She must get away and avoid any more close encounters.

CHAPTER 19
DUAL FRONT

Joey pressed on. She slowed her pace a little. Continuing on down the dirt path, Joey hoped to put some mileage between her and the distant voices. Small tree branches were swiping at her face and ripped her skin. Joey's body began to complain but she forced herself to keep moving. Her strength was draining. Rocks in the path made it difficult to keep her footing. Still she continued to run. An eternity of running passed until she felt safe enough to slowed to a walk. With the deceleration of her feet, her mind became more active.

I wonder if Jesse has awakened from Rachel's little surprise. His senses must be dulling. Could he have mobilized his team so quickly for this chase? One thing for sure, Jesse will be after me just as soon as he possibly can. The Major probably offered him a promotion if he could bring me back. Jesse will hunt me until he captures me or until I'm dead.

Of course, now there's the new enemies that I just made. The Underground dissidents could be those voices just as easily. My experience with them is small. Therefore, their moves will be unpredictable. Would they really shoot me on sight? Or would they bring me safely to rendezvous with Grandmother and Grandfather? There would be enough time to worry about them if they catch up with me. Now is the time to concentrate on finding food, water, shelter, and above all regaining strength.

Fate seemed to smile on Joey for the moment. A storm was brewing over head. Soon the rain would wash away her tracks and make it harder for either group to follow her. However, the storm would bring its own set of problems, i.e. need for shelter, slippery trails, etc. The rain began to fall.

Whichever enemy it is, they will need to stop and find shelter from this driving rain as well. The rain and the darkness of the forest will make it unwise to travel until the rain lets up.

The rain pelted Joey's body, quickly soaking her to the skin. Shelter of some type and warmth were now the highest priority, or mother nature would claim her as a victim.

Joey came to a halt and stood on the trail momentarily. It impossible to see more than a few feet in front of her. Nothing seemed to be moving except the rain drops. The leaves were too wet to use as insulation. Joey moved off the trail searching for a hollow tree trunk that she could use as a shelter. Moving too far off of the trail was dangerous. The darkness of the storm hid the perils that might be awaiting her. She decided a few yards off of the trail would work. She slipped over the inclines from tree to tree. Shortly, Joey was able to find what she was looking for. The trunk was very small, but it would serve her purpose. She squeezed into the trunk and found some dry leaves. There was not as many as she had hoped for, but the leaves would help prevent some of the loss of body heat.

Her stomach growled with hunger, and her throat was dry, but she did not have much at her disposal. Survival training and eating off the land were certainly options, but she was not quite that desperate. Using some of the wet leaves, Joey gathered a few drops of water to drink.

With at least this need abated, she settled down to rest waiting for the storm to end. The sound of the rain pelting the leaves had a tranquilizing effect. Joey found herself dozing off from exhaustion.

Joey awoke several hours later in panic. The rain had stopped and slivers of sunlight peaked through the tree branches. She did not know how long ago the rain had stopped, but she knew it was time to get moving. Moving without caution would draw too much attention. Joey slowly crawled out of the tree trunk and stretched her cramped muscles. She shook the leaves out of her clothing and managed to stand to her feet.

A movement in the shadows caught her eye and made her heart race. Anxiety surged through her body as quickly as the blood in her veins. Outside the safety of the tree trunk, Joey had no place to hide. Her eyes darted around circumspectly. Again another movement in the shadows grabbed her attention.

Is it an animal or an enemy?

Joey could not wait to find out. She would need to keep going. It would be more difficult to catch a moving target. Staying here, she would be a sitting duck. Joey tripped over a few tree roots in her haste to move down the incline back to the trail. The density of the forest gave her no choice but to follow the trail.

Whatever shadow was, it was moving towards her. Was it the deer she had seen earlier? She needed to distance herself from the shadow in the event that it was not. Joey started running away from the last spot she had seen the shadow.

Forced into running again, Joey kept her eyes glued to the path. She was jumping over the rocks and splashing through the puddles. If her pursuers got this far, they would have little difficulty tracking her. She created instant signs as her feet touched the mud. Joey continued running. With her eyes on the path, Joey ran into a large tree limb hanging low over her path. The branch knocked her off of her feet into the mud.

She shook her head trying to clear the stars from her brain. Her fingers found the bump on her head, and she rubbed it instinctively. Blood trickled down into her eye, she wiped it away and forced herself to her feet. Splashing in the mud, she struggled to stand. Her clothing was covered in mud.

As she stood up, Joey heard what she thought was the snap of a gun safety being released. Glancing in the direction of the sound, she saw a large man holding what appeared to be an antique shot gun. The man did not appear to be a member of the Militia. She could not be sure if he belonged to the Underground or not. It seemed rather unlikely.

He pointed the gun at her. He motioned for her to raise her hands. Joey believed that the man was probably the shadow that was following her. She stared at the gun and back at the man. He appeared to be in his fifties. His shoulders were hulky, possibly an elderly body builder. His face was weathered with the stubble of a gray beard. His clothing resembled a hunter's.

I wonder if he had been after the deer I saw earlier.

In life and death situations it was automatic for her programming to take over. She began analyzing the man, the gun and the environment. Joey weighed the probability of the man using the gun. The look of determination on his face said that he would use it. She had no choice for the moment but to obey. Joey slowly raised her hands.

Who is this stranger? If he is not a member of the Militia or a member of the Underground, then what does he want with me?

CHAPTER 20
UNEXPECTED ADVERSARY

The stranger shoved Joey along at gun point away from the trail and through the woods. The terrain was difficult to walk over. The mud pulled at her boots, the thorns ripped at her clothes, and the tree roots tripped her. She probably could have taken the man without much difficulty if her strength was not waning from all she had been through the past week or so. Unsure of who else may be lurking near by, Joey kept a constant vigil. For all she knew, Jesse and his group could be watching. Or possibly the Underground Movement.

Was he friend or foe? What does he intend to do with me? He must be a foe. You don't point guns at friends. What does he want with me?

They walked a long time in total silence until they came upon a dilapidated shack. Joey scanned the area trying to discern some type of landmark in order to get her bearings, but there was nothing to identify the area -- only trees as far as the eye could see.

Entering the shack, she glanced around the room quickly. Joey hoped to get a lay out of the room to use it to advantage at some future point. It was crowded with old newspapers, dirty dishes, and unidentifiable clutter. A few pieces of furniture filled in between the litter around the room. There was a door to what may have been another room or possibly an additional exit. Joey spotted a small cage in the opposite corner of the room.

The stranger shoved Joey in the direction of the cage. Now Joey had enough and decided to fight back. She spun around with a kick aimed at the man's head. The foot found its mark, but it did not seem to affect the man. He stood like a brick wall.

155

That kick should have knocked him off completely off his feet. What kind of a human was he? Maybe he is not human.

The stranger raised the butt his gun and hit Joey in the chest. She collapsed to the floor gasping for breath. He picked her up by the shirt collar and dragged her into the cage and locked her inside.

Panic gripped at her throat as she gasped for every mouthful of air that she could possibly get. The stranger pulled up a chair outside of the cage, sat on it backwards and starred at her. His expression had not changed since their encounter.

After what seemed to be an eternity, Joey could finally take a breath with ease.

"Who are you?" Joey demanded as she scrambled to her feet.

You cannot be intimidating if you are lying down. It is especially important that he understands that I can be intimidating.

The stranger remained silent and continued to stare.

"Are you deaf? Answer my question!" Joey commanded.

Still, no response.

How dare you not answer me? Don't you know who I am? I'm a member of the Militia!

"Who are you? What is the meaning of this?"

There was still no indication of the stranger's intentions.

Not too many people were sympathizers with the New Order, especially way out here. Perhaps he's a member of the Underground. If that's the case, then perhaps he can be intimidated into releasing me.

"I am Lieutenant Joey Benson of the army of the New Order's Militia. I demand that you release me immediately or you will face severe repercussions."

The stranger smirked and finally spoke. "I don't give a damn about your rank or the New Order. You don't intimidate me and neither does your kind." He spoke with a back wood's accent. He leaned his chin on his arm on the back of the chair and continued to stare.

"Are you with the Underground?" Joey asked with a gentler tone. Perhaps he would speak freely if she used a softer tone.

"I don't know anything about any Underground."

Joey seemed puzzled. *He doesn't fear the New Order, and he does not claim allegiance with the Underground. What's his angle? I did not think there was anyone who did not side with one or the other.*

Joey paced around the cage, but continued to maintain eye contact with the stranger.

"Hungry?" The stranger broke the silence.

Two can play this game! I do not need to speak to him either. It did not matter what the subject. I can be silent and stubborn as well and perhaps even better.

Joey glared at the man.

"Sure, you must be! Know you didn't eat the whole day. Nothing fancy out here. Have some dried venison." The man stood up and opened a cupboard and pulled out a piece of venison and tossed it into the cage. "It ain't much, but it'll fill the hole."

Joey followed it with her eyes as it flew into the cage and to the floor. Her stare returned to the man. She refused to follow the food like a dog.

"Go'n! Eat!"

Joey looked at the food and then back to the stranger.

"Suit yourself!"

"I want answers! I want out of here!" Joey broke her silence. "What do you want from me?"

The stranger returned to his chair.

"What I want? Why are you so worried about what I want? . . . . Okay, if you are so interested in what I want, I'll tell you. What I want really is nothing too difficult. You see, I live here alone with little to distract me. All I want are some of life's basic pleasures."

"What?" Joey eyed him suspiciously.

"They really shelter you in that New Order of yours, I suppose? Guess that's all your Militia training. All I want from you is for you to drop your pants from time to time. Give me a little looksey now and again. Nothing very big." The man smirked again. "I keep you here a few days. You entertain me. Maybe even a picture or two, and then you can go."

Joey's eyes widened. "You're sick!"

"I've had a few others here before you. They cooperated and eventually they were on their way. I don't go near them. Lookin' is all I do."

"You're really a very sick man. Have you thought about getting help for this problem?"

"You can think what you wish, but unless you cooperate you'll stay in that cage until you rot." The stranger rose to his feet, winked at her and then exited through the second door. Joey was left alone. Fear threatened to take control of her, but her programming was stronger.

Joey remembered those who failed inspection. The Major humiliated them by making them remove their clothing and stand there naked. She remembered being forced to watch her compatriots and yet disobeying by fixing her gaze on the wall. Perhaps like this stranger the Major got some sick pleasure from seeing young people in this manner.

"No!" Joey said audibly to help her strengthen her resolve. She would not give this stranger his wish. Besides the feeling deep inside her that his was wrong, Joey knew it could make her extremely vulnerable.

She was determined to find a way of escape.

CHAPTER 21
FACING THE ENEMY

The windows of the shack were covered with roofing paper which kept out the sunlight.   Without the sun, Joey had a hard time determining the passing of time. The stranger would come into the room periodically carrying his bottle of homemade liquor, sit on the backwards chair, and stare at her. She was afraid to sleep, even when he was out of the room.

I do not know what he is capable of, especially if he does not get what he wants.

"C'mon, what harm can it cause? Just drop your pants, let me drool a little, and I'll leave you alone for awhile."

Joey glared at him. She positioned herself on the opposite side of the cage at the farthest point away from the man. This would give her room to spring if she needed to.

"Why must you be so uncooperative? I know all about your training. They brainwash you to think that every person is the same. They're wrong! Men and women are different."

Joey looked in disbelief.

How could he know about the training and brainwashing?

"Have you looked at your body lately? You look about thirteen or fourteen. Your body is changing as nature intended."

"Shut up!" Joey screamed. As soon as the words left her mouth, she knew it was a mistake.

I should not betray my feelings this way.

The stranger followed the same routine regularly.

"You don't need to be afraid of me. I said I won't hurt you." The man said as he raised the bottle to his mouth and the liquid ran down his face. "I just want to see and take some pictures when you're gone."

"Right! You bring me here at gun point. You hit me with the butt of your gun. You throw me in a cage like an animal. But you won't hurt me right? Like I believe you! You sit there so smug and smirky." Joey felt her boldness increase. "You don't tell me your name or where your loyalties are. I guess perverts like you are like that."

"Don't call me that!" The stranger growled. Joey's words caused the man to react.

Her programming was dictating her actions. She pressed on, probing what seemed to be a vulnerable spot. Maybe she could get him angry enough to open the cage. Anger blinded other senses. That could all work in her favor for a means of escape.

"What's your problem? Can't get a woman? Perhaps no woman would want you? Only perverts go after someone much younger."

"Stop it!" The man screamed. He jumped to his feet and slammed his fist on the table.

The programming offered no common sense in its tactics. It just thrust Joey forward. The teachings of the New Order ignored danger. Those who are superior are able to handle any danger or threat that may occur or so they were told.

Joey continued needling the stranger and each statement drove him further into a blind, drunken rage. Suddenly, the man seemed almost crazy, as he rushed toward the cage, unlocked the door, and flung it open. His eyes blazed with anger.

Panic seized Joey. Her fear and programming started a war with each other and her guts paid the price. Joey cautiously watched for an opportunity to get past the stranger and out of the cage.

With the man only a few feet away, his breathing was visibly heavy. He lunged toward her. She managed to block his charge. When she tried the flying kick, she hit him and fell to the ground. The man was like a brick wall. He did not even stagger back.

Joey scrambled to her feet. The man grabbed Joey and shoved her backwards. She clumsily fell to the floor. The man attempted to climb on top of her.

"You asked for this!"

"Leave me alone!" Joey shouted as she got her hands up to try to shove him off. The alcohol he had consumed made him off balance. Joey to hurried to her feet.

"I was content to just look, but no, you wouldn't cooperate." He slurred. "Now, I plan to take more than a look."

The man seemed to be obsessed by one thought. A thought that Joey wanted no part of.

It doesn't matter what I say. He's out of control.

"I thought you never touched anyone." Joey shouted. She continued to spar with him. Joey was trying to maneuver towards the door, but he stood firm between her and the exit.

The stranger grabbed her and flung her against the rear wall of the cage, then pressed himself against her.

"Get away from me!" Joey hissed as she mustered all of her strength and managed to shove him back a foot or two.

He was unrelenting. He pushed her back to the wall and pressed up against her again.

"No!" The fear and programming forced the adrenalin to pump overtime. This time she was able to shove the man back far enough to slide away from his grasp. He chased after her. This time Joey whirled, faked a kick to the head, but planted her foot against his chest, taking his breath away and knocking him to the floor. She ran for the cage door. Freedom beckoned her.

She answered the call. She hurriedly slammed the cage door after her. Joey hoped it would lock automatically, making the stranger its prisoner. She dashed for the front door and flung it open only to come to an abrupt halt.

CHAPTER 22
RUTHLESS ROBOTS

Joey came face to face with Jesse Burrows. She gasped.

"Well, Well, Well! If it isn't my dear, old friend Benson. Hanging out in the woods and taking up with strangers? Thought you were taught better than that. It's been so long since I've seen you. I was beginning to really miss you." Jesse's words were thick with sarcasm.

Joey gulped at the sight of him.

Perhaps a quick step could get me past him and then it would be a foot race.

With a quick glance behind Jesse, Joey noticed there were at least six or eight members of his team and waiting for her to try something.

That ends that plan!

"Move back inside the shack!" Jesse ordered.

Joey paused a moment and then decided to comply. She needed a plan. She needed time to develop a plan, but there was not much time. Yet, it would be fruitless to attack Jesse and his team without a plan. Joey backed slowly into the shack keeping her eyes fixed on Jesse. She occasionally glanced behind her to check for obstacles.

Jesse followed into the shack. He was joined by two members of the team. The others probably took up positions outside to cover any attempt at an escape.

"Who's your playmate, Benson?" Nodding toward the stranger in the cage.

Joey kept silent and glared.

The stranger struggled to his feet to face the intruders. The cage door had locked him inside, so he was not a threat.

Jesse closed the door behind him. The two team members stood on either side of him.

"You ran away before we finished our business." Jesse announced. "I'd finish it now, but I've got orders to capture you and return to base as soon as possible. Major Doyle is anxious to see you. Seems he has an appointment for you in his inner office. I suggest you don't resist. You'll need all of your strength for your destiny."

"Why, because resistance is futile? Do you have any other phrases that you want to throw into the speech? I know them all. They're empty words, and the only thing you know to do with them is repeat them." Joey announced sarcastically.

"I'll ignore your bit of sarcasm." Jesse stepped closer toward Joey. "It seems that the New Order is not too sure of your ability to stay a prisoner, so they've given me permission to use a wonderful little device they have developed for problem prisoners."

He pulled an electronic device out of a pouch that was attached to his belt. "This is a proximity device. The Major insisted that I bring it along just for you."

Joey stared at Jesse.

What is he talking about? I never heard about a proximity device being developed by the New Order. Wonder where they got such a thing?

"Richards and Smith are going to attach this to your body. I wouldn't try to resist them if I were you. They've been on their daily doses of vitamins given by the New Order. Unfortunately for you Benson, you have not had the same benefit."

Joey stared at him. She could not believe the calm tone in his voice.

Jesse signaled Richards and Smith to move towards her. Her programming forced her to resist them. To give up without a fight, would be against every bit of her training. It was a reflex. She placed one foot back to equalize her weight and stood waiting for the attack.

Jesse chuckled to himself and said, "You never take my word for anything, do you? I should have expected as much. I'd probably do the same thing."

Joey ignored Jesse's words and focused on the two soldiers moving towards her.

The guards moved towards Joey. Her eyes darted back and forth trying to

164

anticipate their movements. As they moved closer, her muscles tensed. Waiting for the strike was one of the hardest tasks. Timing was everything.

Smith reached for Joey's arm. Shoving it aside with her left, she swung at Smith with her right. Punches and kicks erupted from all parties. Blows hammered Joey's body. Her will managed to keep her on her feet. The fight continued for what seemed like forever.

A blow to Joey's head finally knocked her to the ground. Smith and Richards quickly seized the opportunity to finish carrying out their orders. Joey struggled, but she was not able to free herself from their grasp.

Jesse laughed. "Not bad for someone who's been out of the Order for a while." Jesse walked closer to the group. "Lift her shirt!"

Richards and Smith lifted her shirt exposing her stomach. Jesse took the electrodes connected to the device and attached them.

"The electrodes will burn until they integrate with your body. This device will insure us that you stay between two and six feet from our little party. We're going to be very close for a while Benson. Aren't you touched?" He laughed again.

The electrodes at first felt cold to her skin, and then they burned like fire. Joey knew that every process had to be torturous. The Militia would have it no other way. Her muscles tensed in reaction to the burning. Her will forced her to not cry out at the pain. Once the electrodes became calibrated to her body, they ceased the burning. Her muscles relaxed slightly. The two guards released her and she fell to the floor.

Jesse stood towering over her with his usual smirk. Jesse looked at his watch then ordered, "There's no need to cuff her. She's not going any place except with us. Let's go!"

"If you think I'm going any place with you, you're sadly mistaken." Joey said defiantly.

"Must you always do things the hard way?" Jesse walked toward the door leaving Joey slumped on the floor. "Suit yourself!" When the distance increased to six feet, Jesse turned. "This is six feet. Want to change your mind?

Joey refused to move.

Jesse shrugged and took another step.

Instantly, intense pain spread through every part of her body. She jerked uncontrollably. Joey cried out in response to the intensity of the pain.

Jesse took a step back towards her. "I warned you! With that demonstration over, do you think we can move out?"

Joey nodded and bit her tongue but not before her emotions betrayed her.

There had to be some way to beat this device. Patience would be a necessity. Any plan would still be a guessing game. Possibly my only hope would be to somehow get the mate to this device away from Jesse, but how? That thing will not let me within two feet of him.

Jesse led the way, with Joey following a couple of feet behind him. The other members of his unit fell into position surrounding her. They began the long march back to the Militia's headquarters.

She had to admit this device certainly made transporting prisoners much easier. Joey trudged on.

Is this really the end? Am I defeated this time? Has my luck run out? Have I really blown it or what? I could be safe with Grandmother and Grandfather by now. If I hadn't been so stupid and tried to save that loathsome private in Major Doyle's office, I'd be free now. Enough of this! I must focus on the present. This new device presents a challenge all its own. Are there any options left? If so, what are they?

Jesse continued down the narrow path that Joey had traveled not too long ago.

Maybe I should just end it all? Deprive the New Order of its prize. With me dead, Jesse would be severely punished for failing in his mission. Major Doyle would have his hands full trying to quiet the rumors that would establish me as a martyr. Maybe by using this special device of theirs, I could kill myself and end my torment.

Ending it all would not be the answer for Joey. Her survival instincts were too strong. The New Order had paid great attention to honing that ability. Suicide would never happen.

There had to be another option.

The little band continued trudging down the narrow path. The sun was beginning to set. Soon it would be too dark to continue.

"Guess we'll make camp here." Jesse announced.

166

The group came to a halt. "Richards, Smith, go find some firewood!"
Joey was surprised at Jesse's cockiness.

No leader would build an open fire, knowing the possibility of hostile groups in the area. But Jesse is so self assured, he does not think anyone would ever attempt to ambush or challenge him or his unit.

"Why don't you sit awhile Benson? Make yourself comfortable!" Jesse's voice dripped with sweet sarcasm.

Joey knew it would be useless to resist at this time. She sat on a log and stared at Jesse.

I wish I could shove his smugness right down his throat.

"Benson, I know you wish you could get a piece of me. Personally, I wish I could rip you into little pieces, but I have my orders to bring you in alive and in one piece. And, I obey orders to the letter."

"Yeah right! Just like you obeyed my orders while you were under my command."

"And you've been on my back about that ever since." Jesse shouted.

Joey had gotten a verbal jab in. Jesse was not ready for a verbal assault, but for now it would have to be her only means of attack.

"Furthermore, if you were half the soldier and officer that you pretend to be, we would not be out here in the woods catching our death of cold, having this conversation. You should have delivered me to the Major after our encounter at the Underground's hideout. You're nothing! You let a puny little resister get the better of you."

Joey pushed on. "You're nothing but a robot. You have a tape recorder for brain. You're a programmed puppet of the New Order, more specifically, Major Doyle's."

Joey could see Jesse's jaw muscles tighten.

I'm getting to him. Perhaps if I can anger him enough, he will kill me and put me out of my misery.

"You're so incompetent. You have to rely on a mechanical device to keep me from getting away from you. Seems to me, I must be the superior one." Joey continued to pick at him.

Jesse snorted and was about to lash out, when Richards and Smith returned with the wood. It was enough to distract him, so she would have to wait for another opportunity.

Joey held her tongue while the fire was prepared. She surmised that the other four were probably in the shadows keeping watch.

Four thuds in rapid succession caught everyone's attention. Jesse motioned to Richards and Smith to draw their weapons. Her eyes darted from one person to the next and then into the direction of the thuds. The only noises she could discern were Jesse's heavy breathing and the chirping of crickets.

"Drop your weapons!....You are surrounded!" A voice called to the party.

"Your bluffing, no one is able to get the drop on Jesse Burrows." Jesse shouted defiantly. "You don't have enough fire power to take us."

Click, click, click . . . Joey heard the sounds of dozens of weapons preparing for firing. The sound was unmistakable.

Jesse's eyes widened with the realization that the sounds were a large platoon of soldiers hiding in the shadows. He had been careless, and now he was furious.

"Drop your weapons!" The command was repeated.

"Identify yourself!" Jesse demanded, trying to sound like he was still in control.

"You are in no position to demand anything." The voice responded. "Drop your weapons!"

"No!" Jesse yelled in defiance.

A flash of light. Zip. Richards feel to the ground with a thud.

Jesse rubbed his mouth nervously as he stared at Richard's motionless body. Smith dropped his weapon and raised his hands.

"Don't shoot!" He cried.

"You coward! Pick up that weapon!" Jesse shouted in anger. Smith made no movement toward his weapon. Jesse was so furious when people ignored him. He shot Smith himself.

"Nobody disobeys me!"

Joey stared in terror at Jesse. He was showing his wild and vicious side once again. This was the person that she knew all too well, the side of him that he hides from most everyone else.

"I'll kill Benson." Jesse screamed. "That's what this is all about, isn't it?" He pointed his weapon at Joey.

She prayed that someone would kill her. Death would put an end to it all, the turmoil, the brainwashing and the inner pain, or so she hoped.

The voice was silent at Jesse's threat.

"You want Benson." Jesse shouted.

Jesse glared into the dark woods trying to discern where the threats were located.

"If you think I'm going to just hand her over to you, you've got another think coming. I've got my orders, and I don't care how many soldiers you shoot."

Still, no reply from the darkness.

"Well Benson, looks like your friends ran out on you." He chuckled to himself, diverting his eyes from the target.

Suddenly another flash of light. Zip. Jesse fell to the ground motionlessly.

"Okay Benson, now it's your turn. Down on your knees!" The voice ordered.

"What?" Joey shouted in confusion as she complied. "I'm the good guy here."

I thought they were here to rescue me, not treat me like the enemy.

Out of the shadows emerged a dozen figures.

"You're a real problem." The voice informed Joey. "I'm tired of sending in the troops to rescue you."

"Then leave me." Joey replied without emotion.

"Don't tempt me!"

She strained to recognize the figures in the darkness. *Rachel.* Joey muttered to herself in recognition.

"You killed them?" Joey asked. "After all that garbage about not killing . . ."

"No!" Rachel interrupted. "They're not dead, except for the one he shot. They are all stunned. We have to administer an antidote to the stun within one hour, or they will die. After receiving the antidote, they will sleep for about three hours."

Joey studied Rachel as she spoke.

"On your feet! Let's go!"

"No!" Joey replied.

"I'm tired of fighting with you, just get on your feet and move out so we can deliver you to your grandparents. Now let's go!"

"No, I can't."

"Look, we can sedate you too. It'll be far less problematic for us."

"Will you listen to me?" Joey blurted out in panic. "They've got a proximity device implanted on me. I can't move more than six feet from Jesse."

Joey ripped open part of her shirt.

"Oh!" Rachel replied sheepishly. She bent down with a light to examine the device. "There's a lot of redness around the electrodes. The device appears to be one with a nasty kick. Who has the receiver?"

"Jesse!"

Rachel motioned for one of her people to search for the device. He retrieved a small box from Jesse's belt.

"What's the range on this?"

"I think he said no closer than two feet and no farther than six."

Rachel examined the receiver and suddenly smashed it on the rocks.

"What did you do that for?" Joey shrieked fearing and bracing for the pain, but no pain came. She stared at the crushed transmitter in disbelief.

"Now, let's get moving!" Rachel ordered.

One of the people with her cleared his throat and nodded toward Joey.

"Put her in chains!" She ordered.

"What the . . . "

"We're tired of rescuing you. I don't care if it is because you're ignorant and don't know which people are trying to help you. If it wasn't for your grandfather, we wouldn't bother. We'd let the New Order have you. You're too dumb to know there are some people who really do want to help you."

The guy locked Joey's hands together.

"Now let's go!"

CHAPTER 23
WARS RE-FOUGHT

Joey trudged along behind Rachel, surrounded by the Underground guards. She choked back the panic that was gripping her insides caused by the feeling of being closed in. She did not like being closed in.

It was obvious they did not trust her. Suspicious looks, leery expressions all gave credibility to her impression.

How can I explain to them why I acted the way I did? If Rachel is truly a defector, she should understand what is going on with me. How can I explain why I compromised one of their main escape routes?

Suddenly, a strange sound snapped her away from her pondering.

What is that sound?

She searched the files of her mind for some frame of reference. Finally, it dawned on her.

It's laughter. When was the last time I heard anyone truly laugh? Everyone stopped laughing a long time ago in the New Order.

Their ranks passed a small group of children playing in what appeared to be a park. They certainly were laughing a lot and having a good time. It was obvious they were no longer in the realms of the New Order. These children were dressed in bright colors and doing all sorts of silly things. Their eyes sparkled with delight. Something the children of the New Order were not allowed to do.

One of the guards reached over and freed Joey's hands.

Freedom! I'm out of the reach of Jesse Burrows and the New Order.

Things became a little fuzzy. Joey touched her face, and it felt hot. Maybe that redness Rachel mentioned was an infection. Her feet stumbled and everything went black.

The next thing she could recall was voices fading in and out. Their words all seemed garbled. Instinctively, Joey touched her stomach. The New Order's farewell gift was gone and in its place were bandages. Relief overwhelmed her. She fell back asleep.

Finally, Joey found the strength to open her eyes. When she did, there stood her grandmother and grandfather. Her eyes brightened with recognition, but her programming would not allow her feelings to show.

Both of her grandparents had made it to safety. The Matthews twins had been successful. She made a mental note to acknowledge them in some way for this feat.

Her grandparents expressions portrayed their usual smiles.

"Hi Joey!" They said in unison.

Grandmother continued. "How are you? We're so glad they brought you back to us. We thought we might not ever see you again. After all that you went through, I thought you weren't going to make it."

"We thought Major Doyle had gotten you." Grandfather announced.

Joey continued studying their faces. She waited for the reality of their presence to sink in.

"After we take you home, it will be like old times." Her grandmother chimed in.

Joey looked at her in puzzlement.

It will never be like old times. There is no such thing as old times anymore. Too much has changed.

"We want to help you all we can. If you give us a chance, I'm sure we can understand what you've been through and then we can help you readjust to normal life." Her grandfather added confidently.

They'll never be able to understand. That realization hurt her more than all of the tortures of the Major.

No one will ever be able to truly understand. Perhaps it isn't fair to expect them to understand. Was it fair to expect anyone to understand her torment? Maybe Major Doyle was right. Sharing pain is a weakness that will consume you.

"As soon as you regain your strength, we can take you to our new home in the country." Grandmother beamed.

Joey nodded.

Days passed. Her strength slowly returned, but her mind could find no rest. Before long, they were leading her to their new home.

A deep emptiness had settled inside of Joey. The time spent being indoctrinated by the New Order had caused a great chasm within her, not to mention the division between her and anyone else.

Is there anything that can fill the void? Grandmother and Grandfather care. They even say they love me. Whatever that means! Where do I belong? Where do I fit in? Maybe I'm just a misfit.

Joey knew down deep inside that there was no one she could turn to and say, "Look, this is what I had to go through! Can you help me?" This realization plunged her into a deep depression.

Even when she encountered people on the streets where her grandparents lived, Joey felt they looked at her as if she was from a different planet.

People would whisper and point towards her. "Baby killers! Women haters!" Some would dare say loud enough for them to hear.

"You're one of them!" Another shouted as he jabbed his finger toward Joey's face.

Looking baffled at the accuser's finger, she groped for a response. "I...I...I didn't choose . . . " Her voice trailed off.

What good would it do?

The heckler responded by spitting on Joey.

On her chest sat a big gob of saliva. Joey was so stunned she could not even wipe it away. She stood there watching it as it ran down her shirt and was absorbed into the material.

Why would he spit on me? What did I do to him? I was forced to grow up in the New Order's Militia. I had no choice. I did not volunteer. Why won't they give me a chance?

Standing there, Joey almost wished she were back in the New Order. At least there, she knew what to expect from the people around her. She had thought that life would be different here, that it would be pleasant and good again. Perhaps she might even find a way to fit in, a way to quiet the inner turmoil. The reality of it all was nothing like that would ever happen. Her innocence was gone. She had seen too many things children should never see and experienced things that would make most adults physically ill. As for that little girl, she was lost forever.

Joey spent more and more time alone. She took frequent walks around the homestead in an attempt to clear her mind and lift her spirits, but nothing helped.

I wish I could do as everyone suggests and "Just get over it!" Maybe it would be better to die and get it over with that way.

Joey tried to adjust to the peaceful surroundings of her new home and country. Everyone she met knew she was from the New Order. She could not hide her mannerisms and appearance. Everything about her broadcasted loud and clear that she had been one of the super-soldiers in the New Order's Militia. The people she met were either resentful or afraid of her.

Returning to her grandparents' home, Joey slipped into bed and tried to relax.

Attention all personnel, this area is under attack. Take cover! When Joey awoke, she found herself under the bed in a quiet bedroom. Even sleep did not offer her rest from her turmoil.

Crawling back into bed, she fell into a restless sleep. Charlie visited her dreams as she had done so many nights since the war. Dressed in fatigues, drenched with blood, little ten-year-old Charlie stood there. Part of her head was missing from the self inflicted gun shot. Charlie's voice whispered, "Help me!"

I wish I could forget that horrible day that Charlie died. The memories of Charlie standing there with a gun pointed to her head. As her commanding officer, I should have been able to stop her. We should not have been there to begin with.

Joey thought about discussing her nightmares with her grandparents, but they would not be able to understand the things she experienced. Joey swallowed her frustration and tried to pretend that life in the New Order never existed. This venture was far from successful.

The brain washing and programming methods of the New Order were nearly perfect with their built-in disciplinary procedures. The ultimate goal was for the preservation of the New Order, even if it meant the destruction of the individual. The New Order did not want any loose ends unraveling their close knit program.

The more Joey tried to ignore this programming, the more the inner pain and flashbacks grew. They haunted her every time she closed her eyes.

As time went on, the wars she fought in her mind became more intense than any physical war she had fought in. Every battle was re-fought in her dreams. The intensity of the training films had given her perfect recall of them. Every fight, every battle, and every war was re-fought a thousand times over.

CHAPTER 24
SPECIAL MOMENTS ATTEMPTED

The birds were chirping their songs of joy as Joey awoke from another nightmare ridden night. Her clothing was drenched with sweat. She sat up and wiped her face. Shaking the remnants of war and death from her mind, she straightened her clothing and made her way down the stairs to face another day.

"Hi Joey!" Grandfather said as he set his coffee cup on the table.

"What would you like for breakfast, dear?" Grandmother asked in her usual cheery voice.

Why did it matter what I wanted or did not want for breakfast? Just put the food on the table. Joey left her response unspoken.

Grandmother turned away before she let her countenance fall. She would fix her standard breakfast: eggs and biscuits. Even in their new life meat was scarce. The Bensons were lucky. Their farm had a few laying hens and a cow.

Joey sat at the table in a depressed silence.

Grandfather tried to make conversation, but Joey kept her eyes fixed straight ahead and her voice silent as she sat at attention.

"You can relax a little. It's bad for your digestive system to be so tense." Grandmother said.

"You know Joey, you've been out of the New Order's Militia for over a month now. They're not coming after you. No one is going to harm you. You can loosen up a little." Grandfather informed.

Joey shot him a quick glance, and bit her tongue.

"We want to do everything we can to help you," Grandfather added. "Please let us!"

"We'd like to help you. We hear your nightmares. It rips our hearts apart to see you in such pain, but we can't help if you don't let us." Grandmother pleaded.

"You can't help!" Joey growled. "No one can help. Don't you know the New Order's programming has built a wall inside, and there imprisoned everything. All of the things you call feelings and emotions are a part of what has been imprisoned there."

Their fallen countenances and pained expressions were almost more than she could bare.

"Okay!" She conceded. "You want to help?"

They nodded eagerly.

"I'll tell you about one of the nightmares I've been having. It's about a soldier named Private Charlie Jones. She was in my unit when the New Order went to war. Charlie was a scared little ten year old. As the days of the war wore on, all of the death and mutilated bodies became more than she could bear. One day she snapped and deserted the unit. The unit pursued and eventually overtook her. As the unit closed in, Charlie shot herself in the head and died."

Joey paused and glanced up at their faces.

They were horrified. Neither one of them could find any words to say.

They can't imagine even that one incident. How could they understand the other things; the movies, the humiliation, the torture? That was a mild incident in comparison.

Grandmother, still in shock, set the plate of food in front of Joey. She shoveled the food in without another word. The silence was deafening. It was clear, they would not be able to help. She could not even look at their faces. They meant well, but they did not have any experience to draw upon.

Joey finished eating and left the room. She knew she would eventually be forced to go to school. Some how she would need to find a way to get on with normal living, but what was that? "Normal living" was so far removed, she could not even fathom where to begin.

Most days were rather boring. She would get up have breakfast, wander around the fields, return for lunch, wander around the fields, return for supper, and go to bed. Even in bed, her mind and body never rested. Her stomach felt like it stayed in a constant knot.

Since revealing the incident with Charlie, her grandparents seemed somewhat withdrawn. They gave the usual pleasantries, but did not press her about giving them an opportunity to help. Special moments were no longer attempted. Joey was emotionally alone in a tortured existence.

Her grandparents were still willing to help, but they were just not equipped. If people who cared for her did not have the patience to help her, how could anyone else ever attempt it?

For Joey Benson and others like her, it was either life in this tortured existence, or try to find peace through death.

"Joey!" Grandmother called one rainy afternoon.

Joey emerged from her room puzzled. They normally left her alone unless it was meal time. Entering the kitchen, Joey noticed the grave looks on their faces.

"Joey, we have some bad news for you. Better sit down!" Grandmother continued.

"No thanks, I'll stand!" Joey replied as she clenched her jaw to help set her mind for handling bad news.

"Randy..." Grandmother's voice broke. She began crying. Randy Matthews was special to her. She had helped him through the withdrawals from the New Order's drugs. He, in turn, had safely guided her to freedom.

"Randy Matthews is dead." Grandfather finished.

Joey bit her tongue to divert the possible emotional build up. After a moment she managed to find her voice.

"How?" She said with a flat tone.

"Randy left home a few days ago for a walk, found a gun from some-place, went into the woods and shot himself. The details are a little sketchy. Some hunters found his body yesterday....Joey, I'm sorry. I know he was a fr...."

"He was not a friend!" Joey snapped. "There are no friends!"

"I'm sorry." Grandfather said sheepishly. "He was a compatriot of yours. Randy was such a nice young man."

Grandmother's sobs grew louder.

Joey just stared at a spot on the wall. She was accepting the news like a good soldier of the New Order.

"I didn't know him beyond the time that he helped your grandmother escape to freedom, but we thought the world of him. He was so patient and gentle with her on that long road to freedom. I wish we could have helped him....before it came to this." Grandfather mourned.

"You couldn't have helped him. No one could help him or anyone else from the Militia's Youth army. The sooner you get that through your head, the sooner you'll begin to understand some things." Joey barked. She fought to hold onto her monotone.

Grandmother continued to sob. She was quieter now.

"He's better off being dead. At least for him, the torture is over. Perhaps the rest of us defectors will find the same peace that he has." With those words, Joey stormed from the room.

Her grandparents stared after her in a stunned silence.

CHAPTER 25
FITTING IN?

A memorial service was held for Randy Matthews. Many people attended but few spoke. The compatriots refused to speak or participate because their programming would not allow it. No one else knew much about him. After the service, Joey fell into an even deeper depression.

Why would Randy betray the principles so ingrained in all of us? Suicide is considered the coward's way out. I wonder what went wrong. First Charlie and now Randy, who's next?

"Joey!" Grandmother said one morning at breakfast. "I think it's about time you started back to school."

Joey's head shot up and her eyes fastened on Grandmother in terror.

"I think you have entirely too much time to sit around and brood. You need to be in school. It will help to occupy your mind. Maybe it will even help you to forget about all the New Order nonsense and get on with your life. I should have insisted that you go to school immediately after your arrival here. Maybe you wouldn't have been so gloomy all of the time."

Nonsense! You think what we've been through is nonsense?

"I'm not going. I won't be able to fit in with the kids around here."

"You haven't even tried to fit in. If you truly wanted to fit in, you could begin by taking a regular bath and wearing normal clothes," Grandfather added.

Joey's face burned and her throat ached. "It's not Saturday!" Were the only words that she could muster. In the New Order, the compatriots were only required to bathe on Saturday evenings.

"Joey, you are going to school! I will enroll you today, and you will start tomorrow. This subject is not open for debate. Your grandfather and I believe this will be the best thing for you. Perhaps if Randy had been going . . ." Her voice cracked and she broke off in mid-thought.

Joey bit her tongue. Her training would not allow her to argue her point with someone in authority, nor would it allow her to disobey. Going to school with regular kids would be an additional nightmare.

Dread saturated Joey's heart. The only school she could remember was in the New Order. There discipline was more important than knowledge.

How should I act? What should I say? What will the teachers be like? What will they teach us? Can I fit in?

These questions repeatedly marched through Joey's brain. They stole her appetite and her strength. There was nothing left to do except stay in her room and wait for the inevitable. The questions paraded so fast that she felt dizzy. Once in awhile they crossed in slow motion making her feel sick.

Tomorrow arrived on schedule. The questions disappeared. Joey was on her way to a new school, in a new area, and under a whole new set of rules. Standing in the kitchen, she took a deep breath and started for the door.

"Joey, do you want some breakfast?" Grandmother inquired.

Without looking up, she shook her head.

"You need to eat something." Grandfather insisted.

Joey shot a glare at him, then reached for a grape and shoved it in her mouth.

Grandfather frowned. "I meant something substantial!"

"You said something, and I ate something."

"Must you be so literal?"

"Leave me alone!"

"I fixed you a sandwich for your lunch and an apple." Grandmother said, trying to change the subject. She held out the bag.

Joey snatched it from her hand and moved toward the door.

"Maybe it won't be as bad as you think."

Biting her tongue, Joey continued her journey toward the door.

"Are you going dressed like that?" Grandmother asked.

"How am I suppose to dress?" She looked at the khaki pants and shirt she was wearing. These were part of her. Nothing was going to change that.

"Maybe more like the kids you've seen around the neighborhood." Grandfather added.

"I can't hide who I am." Joey's glare became more intense. "Wearing other clothes won't change who I am. Those kids won't give me a chance, they've already prejudged me." Scaring them into silence, she stomped out of the door.

Her feet dragged as she walked toward the school. Her mind still racing.

What am I going to do if the kids at that school are as bad as the ones who live in our neighborhood? Why are they so prejudiced against me? I haven't done anything to them.

Pictures of the classroom inspection invaded her mind. All of the anxiety over whether or not the Major would find one hair out of place. Woe to everyone if that happened. Everyone standing at attention waiting for the offender to completely undress, finally receiving the Major's nod to resume, and for them to redress. Hopefully, correcting the problem. This would be repeated for each individual offender. Sometimes the morning inspections would drag on for hours.

It's probably doubtful that they'll have an inspection at this school. I wonder what they will have in its place?

Her thoughts were interrupted as she came to a stop in front of a massive, three story, brick building. It reminded her of prison buildings she had seen in their war movies.

This school is huge. The schools in the New Order were all one story.

Kids swarmed across the lawn and funneled through the door. Joey's heart pounded in her ears. Her hands were sweaty and her legs were weak. Her guts told her to flee this situation and live to fight another day.

There would be plenty of other days for school.

Joey shook herself.

Soldiers of the New Order do not allow themselves to feel such things.

Crossing the lawn, Joey entered the building. Once inside, the noise of the hallways drowned out the sound of her pounding heart. Corridors, staircases and unfamiliar door ways spread out as a labyrinth before her.

"Aren't you Joey Benson?" A voice cut through the noise.

Joey startled by the voice whirled around to face its owner.

"Hi! You probably don't remember me, my name is Jackie Swink. I served in the New Order's youth army in C Squadron. I'm the unofficial welcoming committee here at Sugarbush Jr. High."

Joey stared suspiciously at the girl. She certainly did not look like a member of the Youth Army. Jackie was dressed in denim jeans, a tee shirt and sneakers. Her hair length was not regulation. Her appearance did seem to blend in with the rest of the kids there.

"You're staring!" Jackie giggled

Joey blinked and looked away. "Sorry!"

"I know I don't look like I'm from the New Order, but I'm trying to fit in." She gestured to the passing throng.

"Has it helped?"

"Not really! They know we're from the New Order, and they don't trust us. It doesn't matter what we do, they see us as different. Be prepared for some problems."

Joey nodded. "Figured as much!"

"Come on! I better escort you to the office so you can check in. They'll give you a class schedule. If you don't like some of your classes, don't try to change them. They won't let you take anything else and they will think your trying to create trouble. They like keeping the kids from the New Order all together so they can keep an eye on us."

Joey looked overwhelmed.

"Come on!" She headed down a corridor.

Not wanting to get lost in the maze. Joey fell into a quick step behind her.

"There's about six other kids from the New Order attending this school."

They entered the school office and were met by the principal.

"Another kid from the New Order!" The principal mumbled, watching Joey snap to attention in his presence. "Don't salute me!" He snapped. Joey fell into an at-ease position. "I run an orderly and peaceful school here. Don't even think of giving me any trouble. You're here in my school because the law says I have to take you. There's nothing that I can do about that. In time, you'll make me forget where you came from . . . Miss Peterson will give you your schedule."

Joey stared at the principal in disbelief. He had already tried and convicted her as a troublemaker.

What have I done to him?

Miss Peterson wrote down a list of classes and handed them to Joey.

"Are you going to take this one to class?" Miss Peterson asked Jackie.

Jackie nodded. The two former students of the New Order headed for their class.

How can a school be orderly with this much noise? How can anyone learn anything?

Joey had a difficult time keeping up with Jackie. The kids were swarming the halls, all headed in different directions. She was bumped and shoved on all sides. This close proximity to other human beings made her even more nervous.

They finally arrived on the third floor for history class. Entering the room, every eye turned toward Joey. A hush filled the room, followed by a low buzz of whispers. Taking a seat near the front of the room, Joey took a deep breath trying to suppress the mounting panic she felt inside.

Perhaps I have not even dreamed about how bad this whole ordeal can be for me.

Bobby Matthews walked in. This was the first time she had seen him since his brother, Randy's, funeral. He did not seem any different, but no one would expect him to be. He was a good compatriot. Bobby had risked his life to save hers, and she would not soon forget that. She wondered how he was handling the suicide of his brother.

Bobby and Randy were two good soldiers that I could depend upon. Randy will be sorely missed.

Three more kids from the New Order entered. The other class members continued whispering and pointing.

I wonder why they are talking about us. They've seen kids from the New Order before.

Even without the short haircuts or the khaki shirts and pants, they were marked as kids from the New Order. The local kids seemed to not want the kids of the New Order to fit in.

"Why don't you go somewhere else? You're not wanted here." A voice boomed from one of the huddled groups.

"Why don't you go back to your own kind?" Another voice shouted.

"You all should be locked up and the keys thrown away, you're all killers."

Joey's throat ached as each remark bombarded her.

A bell rang and the teacher entered. Joey and Bobby, the only two new kids from the New Order, jumped to their feet and saluted.

The teacher stared at them over his glasses and shook his head. The rest of the class broke into roaring laughter.

Joey's eyes darted around her. No one else was standing. Many were laughing so hard, they were falling onto the floor.

"Class, that's enough!" The teacher instructed. "You two may take your seats . . . This is eighth grade history, not a military inspection. I guess the others of your little group neglected to tell you this little tidbit of information." He stared right at Joey. "I will not tolerate this type of disruption in my classroom. Anyone disrupting my class will pay a most severe price." The teacher droned on.

Humiliation sought to overtake Joey. Taking a deep breath she sat down and lowered her head.

I was not trying to disrupt the class. Don't they know standing is a sign of respect? This is not fair. I do not know the rules here. Will someone please take the time to explain the rules to me?

Every class was the same, even after they stopped jumping to attention and saluting. One of the New Order kids managed to do something during each class that made them a source of ridicule. The disorderly class changes, the loud bells, the crowds, etc. filled Joey with an unmeasurable amount of anxiety.

Things were no better in the cafeteria. The other students threw food and paper at them. Everyone sought to start a fight, trying to prove they were tough to take them on. When Joey refused to fight with them, the kids went to the principal and made false accusations. It seemed they were trying to gang up on the New Order kids when one was separated from the group.

Joey stepped outside to get some air. Before she could inhale, she was surrounded by a dozen community kids.

I guess they think it takes that many of them to beat up one of us.

"We don't want you here. This is our school."

"Why?" Joey asked.

The kids ignored her question and moved closer to Joey. She was not able to fight off a dozen of them. They wrestled her to the ground, kicked her a couple of times in the ribs, and they were gone.

After she was able to catch her breath, she decided not to finish the school day.

If this school does not want me then I do not want to go to this school. I should not be forced to go. Everyone at this school has made it very clear that I am not wanted here. Jackie is a prime example of trying to fit in and she is still not accepted. Therefore, the only logical conclusion is simply not to attend.

CHAPTER 26
STOLEN LOSSES

Mealtime conversations with her grandparents were awkward. Joey tried to spend most meals in silence.

One morning, Grandfather interrupted the breakfast quietness, "Joey!" She looked over the edge of the plate and grunted an affirmation.

"The Underground Movement is having a rally tonight. We are seeking to gather support to send a group into the New Order to infiltrate the dictatorship form of government and possibly overthrow it."

"You're dreaming!" Joey growled.

"You underestimate the power of the Underground Resistance. Look what we did for you and your friends. Who would have thought, we could ever influence anyone to defect, not to mention those that were considered the best of the best."

"First of all, I told you before they are not my friends! Secondly, cockiness will lead to trouble. That's what happened to Jesse Burrows. Thirdly, the New Order is more powerful than you could ever imagine. And lastly, you did not do any of us any favors by bringing us here to be outcasts and end up dying dishonorably."

Grandfather paused a moment to regroup his thoughts. "I'll admit we've made some mistakes, but we need input from young people like you to plan our strategy so we can go back and be more successful. We hope to give courage to some of the people so they will take a stand."

"They'll all be slaughtered!" Joey finished.

"Don't be so negative!" Grandmother chided.

"Negative! You think I'm negative! Perhaps if someone from your generation had done something years ago, the New Order would never have come to power, and we would not be refugees and outcasts now."

"Joey!"

"I'm realistic. You're both living in a dream world. You keep talking like you do, and you'll end up getting a lot of innocent people slaughtered. Life might not be great for them there, but at least they are alive. You stir those people up, and Major Doyle will have no qualms about killing them or worse."

Her grandparents sat in a stunned silence. She did not like quarreling with them, but they just were not being realistic. There was nothing more to say.

"I'm going to school." Joey lied as she left the house. Telling a lie was very bad, but so was going to the situation at school. She had not been back to school for days. If she were forced to go back there, Joey feared for her safety.

I wouldn't mind dying to escape all this pain, but it is not an honorable way.

If her grandparents knew, they would argue with her and possibly order her to go to school. They did not understand the problem. It was better to let them think she was at school.

She was having a difficult time living with a lie.

As she walked, her thoughts drifted back to the last rally she had attended. That one was held by the New Order. Major Doyle used it to intimidate the parents and relatives of the youth army. That was the first time she had seen anyone die in real life. It was also the time Joey discovered just how cold and heartless Jesse Burrows could be, as he watched his own uncle die.

Joey shook off those thoughts and steered her mind toward tonight's rally.

Having such a rally was too dangerous! Didn't Grandfather know there were New Order loyalists everywhere? These loyalists would love claiming honor for themselves with the leaders of the Militia by killing prominent members of the Underground Movement.

Joey did not agree with the dissidents' political views, but she wanted to keep them as safe as possible - especially Grandfather. She continued walking, lost in thought.

"Hey Joey! How ya doing?" Bobby called in a slurry voice and a big smile on his face. He walked with a surreal gait, his eyes were red, and his appearance a little disheveled. A total disgrace for any member of the youth army.

Joey acknowledged him. "You not going to school either?"

"Are you kidding?" Bobby giggled.

"So, what's up?" *What's he smiling about? No one from the New Order ever smiled, especially that broad.*

"Me! I'm up!" He giggled.

"What?" She stared at him quizzically.

"I found a way to escape all those torturous memories, and the pain they gave me. Want me to share it with you?"

"What are you talking about?" Joey inquired, showing a little bit of interest.

"Since we escaped from the New Order, I've had nightmares from the training movies; things that we saw and did during the war; Charlie; and all the other things we went through. I thought I'd go crazy. No one would really listen to what I said about it. My experiences were far beyond their understanding. Sometimes they'd say get over it, you're not living there now. They didn't comprehend how much this was a part of me now." Bobby confided. "Nothing helped! I was at the end of my rope. I even thought about following Randy's example."

"Yeah!" Joey nodded with complete understanding.

"Well, one day I happened to run into this guy, and he had some pills. He said this stuff would make my worries all fly away. I thought, 'I've tried everything else', so I bought them. I went home and took a couple. About fifteen minutes later, I was taking off and before long I felt lighter than air. The guy was right, not one of those awful memories is bothering me."

"You're taking drugs?" Joey asked in shock.

Bobby nodded with a grin.

"How could you? Why would you? What a stupid thing to do!..." Joey groped for words.

Bobby recoiled in surprise.

"Didn't you have enough problems with the withdrawal from the drugs given to us in the New Order? Now you're taking drugs voluntarily." Joey turned her back and walked a couple of steps, then she turned around again.

Bobby stared in silence.

"What happens to the nightmares and memories when the pills wear off? Do you take more? What happens when two pills aren't enough any more to make the memories stay away? Do you take more? What happens then? You might as well waive a white flag in the face of Major Doyle and the other leaders telling them they've won." Joey's voice got higher in pitch and volume as she went on.

"Don't you know other people use drugs? The New Order didn't invent drug use." Bobby defended.

"Drugs are wrong! They're wrong for everyone!"

"Don't give me any of that righteous crap!"

"Other people go through traumatic events, and they haven't bailed out on drugs," Joey quoted her grandfather.

"Haven't you figured it out yet, we're not like other people. We don't experience things the same way as 'normal' people, and we never will. I thought you of all people would understand this. Our feelings have been forced to run deep." Bobby tried to explain. "Our pain runs at a much deeper level. I haven't found anything to reach that deep to ease the pain."

"Drugs are wrong! You shouldn't be using them in any situation!"

"Don't knock it until you've tried it!" Bobby growled. "Besides, maybe I'm not like you. I didn't have the strength to be officer's material, and I certainly don't have it now. So, Lieutenant Joey Benson, seeing that I'm no longer under your command, don't give me orders!" Bobby stomped away.

Joey stared after him in shock. *Drugs! How can he do such a thing? Aren't drugs just an escape from the always-present problems? Drugs seem to be a way to retreat from the problems and even get a respite; on the other hand, drugs strengthen the New Order's death grip on the victim. Isn't standing and resisting the better way to go? Doesn't Bobby understand that? Bobby was always such an eager and cunning soldier. Surely he knows he's killing himself with these drugs. Perhaps his pain is so great that he just doesn't care. And that I can understand*

"It's not the answer." Joey said aloud to herself. She continued to repeat it to herself until she forced the image of Bobby temporarily from her mind.

She returned to her grandparents' house at the time school was dismissed. They were still sitting in the kitchen talking. Their conversation abruptly ended as she walked in the door.

"Don't stop talking on my behalf!" Joey snapped. "I can't imagine that I'd be interested in any topic that you were discussing."

Joey headed for her room without any further words.

"Joey!" Grandfather called after her.

"What?" Joey responded as she turned back toward them.

"I thought you might come to the rally with us tonight."

"Well, you thought wrong. You're nuts if you think I'm going to a dissident rally." Joey felt an inner pain as she realized how disrespectful she sounded, but she chose to ignore it.

"I just thought you might want to come and show your support for the group and thank those responsible for saving your life."

"While I appreciate the work they did to save my life on more than one occasion, in my opinion, they should have let me die. I want one thing to be crystal clear, I have no intention of betraying my compatriots to you or anyone else."

"I just thought . . . "

"Again, you thought wrong." Joey interrupted.

"Would you come and at least allow your presence there to say thank you?"

"No! My presence would give everyone the wrong impression."

"Joey, I want you to come and say thank you to the people that risked their lives for you. Surely you have enough manners left in you to do that." Grandfather's voice betrayed his growing impatience.

"If you order me to come, I'll have no choice but to obey. But I'm not going of my own accord. And I'll let everyone know I don't want to be there." Joey stated matter-of-factly.

"I had hoped that it wouldn't come to this."

"Well, guess what? It has!"

"You leave me no choice. I want you there. I think it is important that you be there. Perhaps by you going and participating, you'll fit in better. Therefore, I am ordering you to attend the rally with me tonight."

"Yessir!" She snapped, saluted and did an about face.

Entering her room, she threw herself down on the bed and punched the pillow repeatedly. Joey continued until she was too exhausted to lift her fist anymore.

Rolling over onto her back, she laid there staring at the ceiling. Images of Bobby and Charlie invaded her mind. The inner pain became even more intense. With her misery growing, she found renewed strength and returned to her punching of the pillow and mattress.

Completely exhausted, she dozed off. She awoke to her grandfather's voice.

"It's time to go Joey."

Joey rose to her feet, smoothed her clothing, as if she were preparing her uniform for inspection. Running her fingers through her still very short hair, she made her way to the kitchen.

When she arrived, both of her grandparents were smiling. She rolled her eyes and followed them out the door to the rally.

Multitudes of people lined the way. Security guards forced the people behind the lines to form a path for the Benson family to walk through. She was amazed at how many people supported the efforts of the Underground here.

She followed her grandparents onto the platform. Everyone was waving and shouting their support for grandfather.

"Thank you! Thank you for your support." Grandfather said as he waved back to the crowd. "I want to thank you all for coming out here to rally against the injustices being carried out in the New Order."

The crowd shouted louder. Grandfather paused, waiting for the noise levels to die.

"First, my granddaughter wishes to express her sincere appreciation for the efforts of the strike force that brought her to freedom and safety."

An unfriendly rumble began to grow from within the crowd. A roar slowly replaced the cheers.

Joey's heart raced. She could feel the tension of the crowd growing. Her eyes darted to and fro. Her uneasiness continued to mount. A feeling of danger grabbed her heart. She was not certain as to why she felt this way.

Suddenly, a stranger rushed to the front of the crowd waving a gun. Joey thought things were moving in slow motion.

"Traitor! Murderer!" He shouted and fired at Joey.

A shot rang out. Instantly, Grandfather leaped in front of her. In that split second, Joey lay on the stage with grandfather laying motionless across her body.

"Grandfather!" She shrieked as they were suddenly surrounded by the security force. A big part of her world just crashed.

CHAPTER 27
LIFE GOES ON

Henry Benson was dead. He died saving the life of the youth known as the prize of the New Order - his granddaughter, Joey.

Why? Why did he do that? Why did he want to save me? Why didn't he just let me take the bullet that was meant for me? Didn't he know that I'd be better off dead? I'd at least be free of the painful memories and the haunting flashbacks.

These lamenting questions filled her mind.

After the shot, Grandmother and Joey had been hustled away from the crowd through back alleys in order to protect them.

"If you had done your job protecting us in the first place, my grandfather wouldn't be dead." Joey complained to the security guards.

They chose to ignore her. In a few moments, the group arrived at the house safely. A pair of guards entered the house first to check it for possible ambushes.

Afterwards, Joey and Grandmother were allowed to enter.

"We'll be keeping watch outside the house." The Captain of the Guard announced to Grandmother. "On behalf of the Security Force Unit of the Underground, let me express my deepest sorrow in the death of your husband." He tipped his cap and left them standing in the kitchen.

Grandmother fumbled for a chair and collapsed into it. She was in shock.

Joey quickly retreated to her room, leaving Grandmother staring blankly into space. Questions returned to her mind, causing the ache inside to rise to high intensity. She turned and punched the mattress and pillow until her hands ached too much to move them. Sometime after Joey stopped punching, she dozed off.

The funeral was scheduled quickly for the next day. The leaders felt that it would be best to have Henry Benson buried as soon as possible.

Why would grandfather sacrifice himself for me? Why did he dive in front of me? How did anyone know that I would be there? I warned both of them that it was a bad idea to bring me. Why wouldn't they listen?

These questions plagued her as she prepared to go to the funeral.

Grandfather's closet advisor, Tom Wilson, was coming to pick them up for the funeral.

A knock on the door, and Tom Wilson was there. He was in his sixties, same as grandfather. They had been friends since before the New Order came to power. Tom had fled to freedom before the New Order sealed its borders.

"Jane! It's good to see you." He said as he entered the house. Giving Grandmother a hug of comfort, he turned toward Joey.

She instinctively stepped away.

"Hi Joey!" He came to an abrupt stop. "It's good to see you too."

Joey nodded.

"Joey, I don't know how to say this."

"What?"

"I...I don't know how to say this, except to just come out and say it. The other advisors feel that it is far too dangerous for you to attend the funeral today! We believe your grandfather would want us to do everything we can to keep you safe."

"What are you saying?" Joey responded in shock.

"I'm saying, you need to stay here where we can protect you easier."

"No! I won't stay here while you bury my grandfather. It's bad enough that your people weren't doing their job and that killer penetrated security. I've been robbed of my grandfather at a time when I need him most . . . " Her voice trailed off. She swallowed hard to force the pain from her throat.

"I understand how you're feeling . . . "

"I don't think you do. My grandfather leaped in front of me, taking the bullet that had my name on it. Now I am being told that I can't even honor him by going to his funeral."

"This is not like the New Order. He's not being processed for food. He'll have a place of honor in the cemetery down the road. You can go pay your respects after the danger passes. The people are a little on edge. Your grandfather would not want you putting your life in danger by going to his funeral."

"It's not the same. I should be there."

"I'm telling you no. You are not to go to the funeral, and that's an order. I'll have one of my men put you in chains if need be."

Joey snapped to attention, saluted, did an about face, and left the room.

"You don't need to do that."

"My men will be here for your protection." Tom called after her.

Protecting or guarding?

Tom and Grandmother left for the funeral.

Anger burned inside of her as she paced her room.

How dare he order me not to go to my own grandfather's funeral? He gave his life for me. I should be there! Why can't anyone understand that?

She continued pacing and kicking or punching any wall or piece of furniture that dared get in her way.

Joey's thoughts turned to another subject.

Why haven't they caught the shooter yet? He was close to the stage. Why couldn't they capture him before he got away? . . . . Unless they didn't want to capture him . . . Unless they wanted him to remain free until he could hit his original target . . . Smells of a conspiracy to me. But, who would want to kill me?

Who's trying to kill me? That's now the question that needs an answer. I'm not going to get any answers being a prisoner in my own house. In fact, I may be a sitting duck in here. The guards already have proven their incompetence. I've had more training than these bozos added together. I think I can give them the slip.

Peeking out the window, Joey did not see any of the guards. Quietly she slipped out the window and headed toward the woods.

That was too easy. Maybe they wanted me to escape, so that I'd be a more explainable target. They could also claim that I took my safety into my own hands, making them innocent of their incompetence.

Looking around, Joey did not see anyone following her. She headed through the woods for the stream.

199

Joey arrived at the stream. An uneasy feeling haunted her. Shoving it aside, she sat down to think. Grabbing a handful of pebbles, she tossed them one by one into the water.

Completely immersed in thoughts about the unknown assassin, a figure was able to approach without her noticing. As the person came closer, the sound of footsteps startled her into the present. Quickly turning in the direction the steps and scampering to her feet, Joey took an attack position. She saw Jackie trotting toward her.

Joey took a deep breath upon recognition.

Jackie came to a halt in front of Joey and glanced over her shoulder in both directions.

"How did you find me?"

"I followed you."

"Followed me? From where?"

"From your grandparents' house."

"I thought those security guards were keeping people away from the house."

"They were out having a cigarette."

Suspicions nudged at the corner of her mind. Joey pushed them aside temporarily.

"Why did you follow me?"

"I have some information for you." Jackie said in a voice that was nearly a whisper. "The left wing members of the Underground have placed a contract on your head."

"On me?"

"Yeah!" Jackie affirmed.

"For what?"

"For the death of your grandfather, Henry Benson."

"What?" Joey screamed. "I didn't kill him."

"Shh--hh! Keep your voice down." Jackie looked around again.

"I didn't kill him." She said again. "That should be obvious to anyone with half a brain. I've got hundreds of witnesses for an alibi. I was on the platform, and he fell down dead on top of me. How could anyone say I killed him?" Joey responded in a lower voice.

"There's no doubt in anyone's mind that the shooter was after you. Because of your position in the New Order,

"FORMER position!"

"Former position means you are still considered the enemy. There are those who believe you are a spy. Other members of the Underground have not forgiven you for betraying one of their best hiding spots on the trail out of the New Order."

"Great! I'm an enemy to both sides."

"They feel that if you hadn't been at that rally, Henry Benson would not be dead."

Joey was troubled by Jackie's last comment. Swallowing hard to relieve the pain in her throat, she managed to find her voice.

"Who are THEY?"

"This left wing faction of the Underground Movement doesn't trust anyone who has held any type of position in the New Order. They are especially opposed to anyone whose loyalty they question."

"Namely mine!"

Jackie nodded.

"Because of my compromising that hiding place?"

Again Jackie nodded. "What do you plan to do?"

"I don't know." Joey sat down. Her body felt drained of strength.

"Whatever you decide, I'm with you and I'm sure I can find some others who will stand by you."

"You? Why? You seem to fit in."

"Not really! I haven't exactly been welcomed here with open arms, even with my efforts to fit in."

Joey nodded with understanding.

"No one knows I've sided with you, so I can slip into key places and gather information."

Joey nodded, and Jackie was gone.

How could they blame me for Grandfather's death? How cruel are these people? Perhaps it was better to live in the New Order? But there is no returning for me.

The pain in Joey's throat ached anew. Her eyes burned, but tears were forbidden. She shook her head hard trying to shake the thoughts out of it.

New thoughts entered her mind. Something bothered her about Jackie. She could not quite put her finger on what it was. Joey let her thoughts drift onto another subject.

It will take all of the resources I can muster from my training in order to survive against a dual enemy. There must be a way to persist. Survival is a must. This all is so unfair! Grandfather, a man of peace was cut down instead of me, a person of war.

None of this is fair. I've faced death many times; I've seen numerous people die, why can't I deal with one man's death . . . I always thought he would live forever. Well, at least he can no longer feel the pain that I brought him.

Retreating to the solitude of her mind, Joey stayed there alone with a hurt no one else could ever understand. Time stood still as the pain engulfed her insides.

Her thoughts were interrupted by the crack of a branch. Joey jumped behind the rocks for cover. Shots rang out.

I'm a sitting duck. I don't even have a weapon.

After about six shots, Joey heard footsteps running away and then more steps toward her.

Joey frantically looked around her for something to defend herself with.

"It's me!" Jackie called as quietly as she could.

Joey breathed a sigh of relief for a moment. Then suspicions came back to nag at her.

It seemed rather convenient that Jackie came along just as a sniper was taking potshots at me.

"Did you see anyone?" Joey asked.

"No! Whom should I have seen?"

"There was someone here taking shots at me."

"It's not safe here for you. We have to find somewhere to hide you. Have you thought about going back to your house? At least there are guards there."

"I don't trust them."

"What other options do you have?" Joey thought a moment and

shrugged.

"I guess I can give the house a try. At least I have walls to help keep them out."

"Let's go!"

Joey walked a step behind Jackie. She wanted to keep Jackie in front of her. Her training commanded her to be cautious.

"What did you find out?" Joey asked.

"I managed to find four more compatriots who want to join up with you."

"To do what?"

"To wage war against those left wingers. You're a born leader. It's time we let people know that we will fight for what we want."

"Who are the compatriots?"

"Bobby Matthews, who you already know. Casey Randall . . . "

"Who?"

"Corporal Casey Randall is a twelve-year old male from squad 'D'."

Joey nodded. "Who else?"

"Private Billy Schultz is eleven years old and is also from squad 'D'. Private Lindsey Kenton is eleven. She's female and from squad 'F'. Corporal Gregory Hinson a twelve year old from squad 'F'. That's your team."

"What else did you find out?"

These were not Joey's first choice for a team. She did not now anything about their deeds or skills. Yet, she needed help. Joey was used to having compatriots around her. Even with Bobby on drugs, he would be better than nothing.

"There's a number of people searching for you. They've been able to influence some of the locals who are also searching for you. We've got to get you some place out of the open."

The two of them continued toward her grandparents' home. Joey was wary of Jackie, but she did not know who else to turn to for the moment.

CHAPTER 28
CASUALTIES OF COMBAT

"Grandmother?" Joey called as she entered the house. She heard muffled sobs coming from the dining room. As Joey entered the room, she saw her grandmother sitting at the table, her head in her hands, and tears running down her face.

"You shouldn't have come back here." Grandmother managed to find the words.

"I came to see how you were doing, besides I thought I could hide here."

"It's too dangerous. Members of the Underground are searching for you. If they find you, they will kill you."

"What about those security guards that were here?"

"They're not here anymore."

Joey pulled up a chair across from her.

"Joey, I love you dearly, but you can't stay here. I don't want to see you hurt or killed. I couldn't bear that. I don't know how to deal with the emotional problems that the New Order has caused you. Your grandfather was so much better at this than me. Maybe you should go live with your mother."

"What are you saying?" Joey said trying to hide the pain in her throat.

"Please understand that it pains me to say this. My understanding of the problems you're experiencing is very limited. I see you falling further and further away from society and from me. I feel helpless. With the authorities hunting for you, it would be safer if you didn't come back here for awhile. Please try to understand this is only temporary....things will quiet down. The danger will pass. We will all adjust." Grandmother said between sobs. "You mother said you can stay with her."

"Fine!" Joey jumped to her feet and stomped out the door. "I know when I'm not wanted."

Joey knew Grandmother was taking the loss of her husband very hard, but she could not understand why Grandmother was turning her away. If there was anyone she believed in it was her grandparents. They had faced some very difficult times before. Why was this any different? If this situation was enough to turn grandmother away from her, then none of it was real.

She desperately wanted to find something to believe in. But what? Nothing seemed real. Her life before the New Order's takeover was a fading dream. Life in the New Order was a nightmare. Her escape to freedom and life since has been a continuous flashback. Now the only people who had ever cared about her were gone.

With Grandfather dead, the little thread of reality that she had clutched had been ripped away. Without solid footing, she had nothing to stand on. What was real? For that matter did reality exist outside of her head? No, the only reality was inside her head and now she wasn't completely sure of that.

Perhaps the Major was right. He said there was no leaving the New Order. It had grown to be a part of her. It was her basis of self-identification. Wherever she went, it would be there too, to torment and mock her, or protect her. You can not win outside of the New Order, they made sure of that. Their indoctrination, brainwashing, and programming methods were too good. There is no escape. The past does not change for anyone.

Outside the house, a figure in the shadows caught Joey's attention. Her heart leaped into her throat. She slipped back inside the doorway. It was becoming more and more apparent that Joey needed to find a weapon of some sort.

Another figure caught her eye. The first figure ran into the darkness of the woods.

"Joey!" The voice was familiar, but she was not sure who it belonged to. "It's me, Bobby."

Joey took a deep breath. "You scared the devil out of me."

"Sorry! I came to warn you."

"About what?"

"Jackie is a spy."

Chills ran up and down her spine.

"A spy for which side?"

"She's a plant from the New Order."

"How did you find out?"

"This guy I know got high, and he talked non-stop."

"Ever think you might do the same?"

"If you want my help, don't start."

"Okay!"

"First thing is to get you to safety. Come on!"

Bobby led the way through the darkness. He was bobbing and weaving across a field.

I wonder if the other figure is following us? I wonder where Bobby's leading me.

She could not help but wonder if Bobby was legit, or if he too was a plant.

Bobby had changed directions so many times, Joey lost count.

I wonder if this is how he was so successful getting grandfather to freedom.

They came to a stop deep in the woods. A lean-to was camouflaged by the trees.

"We'll stay here for now. I'll keep the first watch." Bobby announced.

"Thanks!" Joey sat down inside the shelter.

The long hours of the night passed without incident. In the morning, Bobby was once again leading the way.

"Where are we going?"

"A little remote place where they'll never find you."

"Do you think Jackie was the shooter?" Joey forced herself to say the words. She was charging a compatriot with the assassination of her grandfather.

"She was not. The shooter is another plant; someone that Jackie knows."

They continued talking about the New Order spies.

Arriving at the remote place, they sat down to relax. Looking around, Joey nodded her agreement with the probability that no one would find them out here.

"You came through for me again." Joey said.

"I'm glad I could help, Lieutenant."

"Now what?"

"Well, I for one, need something to help me fly a little."

"You're not!"

"What?"

"You're not going to take drugs."

"Yeah! I'm going to take some pills I got in town. Don't nag me! I got you out of that mess safely."

Joey went to sit by the shore of the nearby lake. She did not want to be around Bobby while he was getting high. Her mind was in a whirl as she tried to contemplate her next move. Joey's thoughts were interrupted.

"Hey Joey!" Bobby shouted. "You really shouldn't knock this stuff. It makes you feel great!"

He was running and jumping around on the rocks that were near the shore.

"Bobby! Shouldn't you keep your voice down?"

"There's nobody out here but the crickets." He laughed and jumped to another rock.

Each jump was more daring than the one before.

"Don't you think you better sit down?"

"No way! I'm invincible."

Bobby leaped for another large boulder. He lost his balance as he landed. In a split second, Bobby fell backwards hitting his head on the rocks.

"Bobby!" Joey screamed as she jumped to her feet and rushed towards Bobby.

Arriving at Bobby's side, she could see trickles of blood coming from his mouth and ear.

"Sorry!" Bobby said weakly.

Joey did not know what to say as she watched him die.

It wasn't his fault. I guess I can understand trying to escape the pain by any means available.

Joey gathered the rocks along the beach and piled them over Bobby's body. Even though there was no declared war taking place, Bobby was a casualty of combat. In that, there was no doubt. Now, he had joined his brother in death and in freedom.

CHAPTER 29
GLIMMER OF HOPE

Charlie...Randy...Bobby. One by one the compatriots she had commanded were failing the test of life. Was it a mistake to rebel against the will of the New Order? Should I have let Jesse brutalize the members of the Underground that night? Would things have been any different? Perhaps I'd only have one enemy then. Perhaps Randy would still be alive. Maybe Bobby would never had turned to the drugs that caused that life-ending accident life. Will I be next? It seems unavoidable.

Between suicide and drug overdoses, they were falling, and with each one Joey felt herself fortifying her inner wall. Her duty was to survive, and she was determined to do her duty. The programming dictated her actions, yet she wondered how reliable it was without constant reinforcement from the New Order. Even if she wanted to ignore the programming, she could not.

Questions remain. Is Jackie behind the death of Grandfather? Is she instigating the attempts on my life? Why? More importantly, what can I do about it?

Falling into a troubled sleep, her mind began to dream.

The stranger had captured her again. "So, you want to impress me by your rank in the New Order." He chuckled. "You know why I think females will never be good officers? You can humiliate them just by pulling down their pants."

Joey sat up. Her heart was pounding and her breathing was quick. Glancing around, she realized that she was in the safety of the shelter that Bobby had guided her to. Taking a deep breath, she made a conscious effort to slow her heart and breathing.

I can't stay here. If I do, I'll go crazy.

At that moment, she decided to go back.

Rachel. I have to find Rachel. She seems to be the only person that truly wanted to help me, but I was too blind to let her. I hope it's not too late.

Joey had not seen Rachel since the march to freedom. But, she was determined to find her.

She started the long hike back to civilization. Then again, what is civilization? It's a funny word. One that can be defined by one's own circumstances. Major Doyle thought the youth army brought about a perfect civilization. The Underground thought that overthrowing the military would bring about civilization. She imagined the assassin thought they were furthering civilization by killing her.

It seems that my only hope is finding Rachel. Yet, would she really help me? Could she even understand what's going on in my head? If she can do that, she would understand me better than I understand myself. Then again, I don't understand myself either. Am I really prepared to face the things that Rachel mentioned: my fears, my nightmares, and who knows what else? Can she help me develop some new dreams and then find the courage to follow them? More importantly, can she help me overcome the programming?

The questions remained without answers.

Joey felt a hint of peace as she resolved to search for Rachel. It was a glimmer of hope in a very darkened life. A spark that she was desperate to hold on to. The glimmers of hope were the lights in Joey's very dark world. She would search out those glimmers until they become spotlights.

I will survive and my victory will be the testimony against the New Order's brainwashing and programming. I will not let them win!

Printed in the United States
22738LVS00004B/210